THE BOLD, BAD BOYS!

and other stories

CLIVEDEN PRESS

Published in Great Britain in 1992 by Cliveden Press,
an Egmont Company, Egmont House, PO Box 111,
Great Ducie Street, Manchester M60 3BL.
Printed in the United Kingdom.

ISBN 0 7498 1226 5

Enid Blyton

Enid Blyton was born in London in 1897. Her childhood was spent in Beckenham, Kent, and as a child she began to write poems, stories and plays. She trained to be a teacher but she devoted her whole life to being a children's author. Her first book was a collection of poems for children, published in 1922. In 1926 she began to write a weekly magazine for children called *Sunny Stories*, and it was here that many of her most popular stories and characters first appeared. The magazine was immensely popular and in 1953 it became *The Enid Blyton Magazine*.

She wrote more than 600 books for children and many of her most popular series are still published all over the world. Her books have been translated into over 30 languages. Enid Blyton died in 1968.

Contents

Well really, Clockwork Mouse!

The clockwork mouse was a good little thing till the day he discovered the old paint-box at the back of the toy cupboard.

"What's this?" he asked the big doll.

"A paint-box, silly," said the big doll. "You get a paint-brush and dip it into water, then you dab it on to one of those paints – and you can paint all sorts of colours with the brush! Leave it alone. It isn't yours."

But the clockwork mouse didn't leave it alone. He thought it was a wonderful thing. You could paint colours everywhere by just dabbing a wet brush on those square coloured slabs in the tin box!

He found a brush. He couldn't find any water so he thought he would lick

the brush to make it wet. And, dear me, when he dabbed the wet brush on to a red paint, and then dabbed the brush on to the wall of the toy cupboard, he made a bright red patch.

"It's marvellous!" thought the clockwork mouse, and stopped being a good little thing from that very moment! He didn't tell anyone, though. He wanted to keep it a secret.

Peculiar things began to happen in the playroom among the toys.

One day everyone stared hard at the big doll, who had been sound asleep and had just woken up.

"What's the matter? Why are you staring?" she asked.

"Your cheeks are blue instead of red," said the baby doll. "You look peculiar. Do you feel ill?"

And then the teddy bear looked down at himself the next day and found that his tummy was bright red. How very, very strange. It had been a nice brown furry tummy, and now it was red.

Perhaps he was ill, too? He felt most alarmed.

"What's happening?" said the toys. "We keep waking up with something strange about us. Are we going to be ill? Is it catching?"

The clockwork mouse giggled to himself in his corner. This was funny. He kept wanting to laugh all the time when he looked at the big doll's blue cheeks and the teddy bear's red tummy.

The next day everyone was staring in horror at the pink rabbit. His pink face was white! Yes, white all over, and he looked really frightening.

"What's the matter?" he said. "Am I blue or something?"

"Your pink face is white," said the teddy bear. "It looks dreadful. What *can* be happening? Is it an illness, or a bad spell, or what?"

The clockwork mouse was thoroughly enjoying himself. He kept licking his brush and getting more and more colours out of the wonderful paint-box.

He was very clever at painting the toys while they slept. Nobody guessed what was happening at all.

Soon the dolls' house had purple walls instead of cream. They looked dreadful. Then the big doll's shoes appeared in pink and yellow instead of white, and the little doll's hat became bright red instead of pale blue. It was all very puzzling.

The sailor doll found that his shoes were brilliant orange one morning, and when he bent down to look at them everyone shouted loudly, "The top of your head is green! It's green! It's very green indeed!"

Well, it wasn't long before everyone had something peculiar about them except the clockwork mouse. The toys expected him to appear in red or blue or yellow one day, but he didn't. He just remained grey with a nice long tail.

Goodness knows what would have happened next if the clockwork mouse hadn't suddenly felt ill. He had been planning to paint the playroom walls with blue and orange, but when he dipped his brush into his mouth to wet it, as usual, he suddenly felt very sick.

He went and lay down in a corner of the empty brick-box, feeling very sorry for himself. The pink rabbit came up to him, with his face still very white indeed. "What's the matter?" he said. "Do you feel ill?"

"Yes, very," said the clockwork mouse. "Very, very."

The toys talked together. They were upset. "Better look at his tongue," said the sailor doll. "That's the first thing that doctors do when anyone is ill."

"Put out your tongue and let us see it," said the teddy bear to the mouse. So he put out his tongue. The toys gave loud screams. It was all the colours of the rainbow!

"It's pink and yellow and blue and green and purple and white . . ." began the sailor doll, in horror. "What illness has he got? What a terrible tongue!"

The big doll stared hard at the clockwork mouse's tongue. Then she pointed her finger at him.

"You bad, naughty, wicked little mouse!" she said. "It's *you* that has given me blue cheeks, and given the rabbit a white face, and the bear a red tummy. You've been using that paint-box! I know you have!"

The clockwork mouse gave a little squeak. "I feel ill. I feel ill."

"And it serves you right!" said the big doll. "Do you know why you feel ill? Because you've been putting that paint-brush into your mouth with all the paint on it, instead of using water as I told you. Now you've poisoned yourself with the paint. It serves you right."

The mouse began to cry. He was frightened. "I'm very sorry. It was a joke. I'm poisoned. Oh, what shall I do?"

"You can just wait till we've all washed off the paint you dabbed on us," said the big doll. "Thank goodness we know what it is! Come along to the basin, everyone, and we'll soon look ourselves again."

Well, the teddy got rid of his red tummy, the rabbit's face came pink again, the sailor doll washed off the green on the top of his head, and the big doll no longer had blue cheeks. They all felt much more cheerful when they had washed off the paint.

"It was naughty of him – but it was a bit funny, too," said the teddy bear. "No wonder I kept hearing him giggling away in his corner. He's always been such a good, quiet little thing. Who would have thought he could be such a mischief?"

"I think we'll forgive him," said the rabbit. "He's feeling very sorry for himself. We'll give him some water to drink to wash the paint off his tongue. Then he'll feel better."

He did, of course, and now he's quite all right again. But would you have thought a clockwork mouse could ever have played such a trick?

The quarrelsome bears

There were once two bears who lived in a little yellow cottage in Toy Village. Teddy was a brown bear and Bruiny was a blue one. And how they quarrelled! Really, you should have heard them!

"That's my handkerchief you are using!" said Teddy.

"Indeed it's not!" said Bruiny.

"I tell you it *is*," said Teddy.

"And I tell you it's not!" said Bruiny.

"Don't keep telling me fibs," said Teddy.

"Well, don't you either," said Bruiny.

That was the sort of quarrel they had every single day. Silly, wasn't it? Especially as they both had more handkerchiefs than they needed.

One afternoon they dressed themselves in their best coats and ties to go to a party. They did look nice. Teddy tied Bruiny's bow and Bruiny tied Teddy's. Then they took their new hats and went to the door.

And it was raining! Not just raining quietly, but coming down angrily and fiercely – pitterpatterpitterpatterpitterpatter, without a single stop.

"Goodness! Look at that!" said Teddy. "We must take our umbrella."

They had a big red umbrella between them, and it was really a very fine one indeed. Teddy looked for it in the umbrella-stand. It wasn't there.

"What have you done with the umbrella, Bruiny?" asked Teddy.

"Nothing at all," said Bruiny, at once. "What do you suppose I've done with it? Used it to stir my tea with?"

"Don't be silly," said Teddy. "That umbrella was there yesterday. You must have taken it out."

"I did not," said Bruiny. "You must have taken it yourself."

"I haven't been out for two days," said Teddy. "What do you think I'd want with an umbrella indoors?"

"Oh, you might use it to smack the cat with," said Bruiny unkindly.

"Oh! As if I would smack our dear old cat with an umbrella!" cried Teddy angrily.

"Well – perhaps you used it to poke the fire," said Bruiny.

"And perhaps *you* used it to scrub the floor!" cried Teddy. "I can think of silly things too. No, it's no good, Bruiny. You took that umbrella for something, and you might just as well try and remember what you did with it and where you put it. Hurry, now, or we'll be late for the party."

"I tell you, Teddy, I haven't had the umbrella and I don't know where it is," said Bruiny. "It would be a good thing if *you* thought a little and found out where you had hidden it."

"I don't hide umbrellas," said Teddy.

"Well, you once hid the cat in the cupboard and it jumped out at me," said Bruiny.

"That was just a joke," said Teddy. "I shouldn't hide our umbrella in the cupboard, because it wouldn't jump out at you."

"But you'd like it to, I suppose?" cried Bruiny, getting crosser and crosser.

"Yes, I'd love to see an umbrella jump out at you!" shouted Teddy, getting angry too.

"You're a bad teddy bear!" said Bruiny, and he pulled Teddy's bow undone.

"Don't!" cried Teddy. He caught hold of Bruiny's coat, meaning to give him a good shaking. But he shook too hard and the coat tore in half!

"Oh! Oh! Look at that!" wailed Bruiny. "I'll jump on your hat for tearing my coat!"

And before Teddy could stop him, Bruiny had thrown his new hat on the floor and jumped on it. It was quite spoilt!

Then they both went mad. They tore each other's ties off. They threw both hats out of the window. They even threw each other's handkerchiefs into the waste-paper basket!

And in the middle of all this there came a knocking at the door! Bruiny went to open it, panting and torn. Outside stood Mrs Field-Mouse with all her little family. They were on their way to the party, each mouse under its own tiny umbrella.

"Goodness me! What's all the noise about?" asked Mrs Field-Mouse severely. "I knocked three times before you heard me."

"Well, Mrs Field-Mouse," said Bruiny, "Teddy has taken our umbrella and doesn't know where he put it."

"Oh, you fibber!" cried Teddy. "It's Bruiny that must have taken it, Mrs Field-Mouse. We've only got one, and it's raining, and we wanted it to go to the party."

"Dear me!" said Mrs Field-Mouse.

"What have *you* come for?" asked Bruiny.

"Well, I came to give you back your big red umbrella," said Mrs Field-Mouse with a laugh. "I suppose you forgot that you both kindly said I might have it yesterday to go home with my little family, because it was big enough to shelter them all. I promised to bring it back today. Here it is. I'm sorry you should have quarrelled about it."

She stood it in the hall-stand and then went off to the party with her little family. How they squealed when they heard the joke!

"Well, I never," said Bruiny, looking at the umbrella. "So you didn't take it, Teddy."

"And you didn't either," said Teddy. "Oh dear, how silly we are! We've got our umbrella – but we've torn our suits and ties and spoilt our hats, so we can't possibly go to the party after all."

"I beg your pardon, Teddy," said Bruiny in a small voice. "I'll make you some cocoa for tea."

"And I beg your pardon, too," said Teddy. "I'll make you some toast for tea. We'll never quarrel again!"

But they did quarrel, and do you know why? It was because Teddy couldn't find the toasting-fork, so he toasted the bread on the end of the red umbrella! Bruiny was so angry, because he said the toast tasted of mud!

Well, well, well! You can't please everybody, can you?

The rabbit who lost his tail

In the playroom cupboard with all the other toys lived Bun the soft rabbit. He was dressed in an orange tunic and green shorts, and his tail stuck out behind. It was a funny little tail, very short and fluffy, just like a real rabbit's.

Bun often played with Mollie, his mistress. She used to take him into the garden with her, and he sat on a little wooden chair and pretended to have tea. He was a very happy little rabbit.

One day a pixie climbed in at the window and gave Bun a letter. It had a crown printed on the back, so Bun knew that it had come from a King or Queen. He was very excited and his

paws trembled when they tried to undo the envelope.

All the other toys crowded round to see what the letter inside was. Bun unfolded it and read it out loud. It was from the King of Fairyland!

DEAR BUN,

I am having a party under the old beech tree on Wednesday night at moonrise. Please come if you can.

Love from

THE KING OF FAIRYLAND.

Bun danced for joy. He had always wanted to go to a pixie party, but toys didn't very often get asked.

"Wednesday!" he said. "That's two days away. Oh, how can I wait?"

Bun was very happy all that day – but the next day something dreadful happened. He lost his tail!

Mollie had taken him out into the garden to play with him and the little boy next door came to play too. But he was rather rough with Bun, and to make Mollie laugh he held the little rabbit up by his tail.

But Mollie didn't laugh. She snatched Bun away from the little boy and scolded him.

"That's not funny!" she said. "You'll hurt Bun. You're a nasty little boy and I don't want to play with you any more."

Then the two began to quarrel, and soon they were shouting at each other loudly. Mother came out and sent the little boy away. Then she took Mollie indoors.

All that day Bun lay out on the grass. The rain came and made him wet. Then suddenly Mollie remembered him and ran out to fetch him. She sat him in front of the playroom fire to dry, and there he stayed in the warm until Mollie went to bed.

Then, when the playroom was empty and quiet, all the other toys crept round Bun to hear what had happened. He told them all about the little boy who held him up by the tail and the toys exclaimed in horror.

Then suddenly the bear gave a squeak.

"Ooh, Bun!" he said. "Where *is* your tail?"

Then all the toys looked at Bun's back, and sure enough his tail was gone. He had no tail at all.

He *was* upset! He turned his head round to look at the place where his tail wasn't, and the tears came into his eyes.

"What shall I do?" he wept. "I can't go to a pixie party without a tail, I really can't. Why, I should feel only half-dressed. Oh, whatever shall I do?"

The toys looked at one another and thought hard.

"I'll run out into the garden and see if I can find your tail for you," said the clockwork clown. "If someone will wind me up, I can easily get there and back."

The teddy bear wound him up and the clockwork clown ran out of the

room and down the passage that led
to the garden. He hunted everywhere
about the grass for Bun's tail, but he
couldn't find it. At last he didn't dare
to hunt any longer for he was afraid his
clockwork would run down, and then
he wouldn't be able to get back to the
playroom.

"Well," said the toys, when he went
back to them, "did you find it?"

"No," said the clown, "it isn't there."

Then Bun wept more loudly than
ever, and all the toys looked at one
another and thought hard again.

"Couldn't one of you lend me a tail?"
asked Bun, at last.

"I haven't got one or I would with
pleasure," said the teddy bear.

"What about the baby lamb that lives
in the toy stable?" cried the clown. "He
has a fine long tail, and I am sure he
would lend it to you."

"But wouldn't I look funny with a
very long tail?" asked Bun. "My own
was so short."

"Oh, a long tail is better than nothing," said the teddy, and all the toys agreed. So they went to fetch the baby lamb from the stable and told him what they wanted. He didn't like parting with his tail at first, but when the clown told him all about the wonderful pixie party that Bun had been invited to, he said yes, he would lend his tail just for that night.

"It's only pinned on," he said, "so Bun can quite easily unpin it and put it on himself."

"Well, I'll borrow it tomorrow, and thank you very much," said Bun, happily. Then all the toys went to sleep, and the playroom was quiet.

The next night the toys fetched the lamb again, and the clown unpinned his tail. It was very long, soft and woolly and felt lovely and warm. Bun turned his back to the clown, and in a trice it was neatly pinned on.

"Ooh, Bun!" said the teddy bear, "you do look fine! A long tail suits you much better than a short one. Everyone will look at you and admire you."

Bun felt very happy. He took his invitation card, said goodbye to the toys and set off to the big beech tree. The moon was just rising, and as he came near the tree he could see crowds of pixies and elves there.

Bun wondered if Tiptoe, the elf who lived in the foxglove bed, was going to the party too. He was very fond of Tiptoe, and he had often wished that she would marry him and live with him in the playroom. But he had never dared to ask her, for she was very lovely.

Suddenly he saw her. She ran up to him and tweaked one of his big ears.

"Hello, Bun!" she said. "I'm so glad you're going to the party."

"Will you dance with me?" asked Bun, in delight.

"Yes," said Tiptoe, and then she sneezed three times.

"Oh dear, you haven't got a cold, have you?" asked Bun in alarm. "What a thin dress you have on, Tiptoe, and the wind is so cold too."

"Yes, I ought to have put on something warmer," said Tiptoe, and she shivered, "but it's too late now. Perhaps I shall get warm dancing."

The party soon began. The band struck up a merry tune, and all the pixies and elves began to dance. The King and Queen sat on two toadstool thrones, and clapped when each dance was finished.

Bun enjoyed himself very much, because everyone admired his tail.

"What a beautiful tail!" they said. "You *are* a lucky rabbit to have a tail like that! How nice you look! Will you dance with us?"

So Bun danced every single dance, and was so happy that his ears turned bright red inside. But he liked dancing best with Tiptoe. He was worried about her because she did sneeze so, and he

felt certain she would get a very bad cold, and be ill.

Suddenly the Queen heard Tiptoe sneezing and she called her to the throne.

"Why didn't you put on a warmer dress?" she said. "You really must go home, Tiptoe, for you will get a terrible cold."

"Oh, please, Your Majesty, do let me stay!" said poor Tiptoe. "A-tishoo, a-tishoo!"

Then a wonderful idea came to Bun. He ran up to the Queen and bowed.

"I can lend Tiptoe a fur to put round her neck," he said. "Would you let her stay if she wears a fur, Your Majesty?"

"Certainly," said the Queen. "But where is the fur?"

"Here!" said Bun, and he unpinned the long woolly lamb's tail! He put it around Tiptoe's neck, and there she was, as warm as toast, and as pretty as a picture.

How all the elves and pixies cheered! They knew that Bun was proud of his long tail and felt very odd without it, and they thought it was very kind and unselfish of him to lend it to Tiptoe and go without it himself.

After that Bun was more of a hero than ever. All the elves wanted to dance with him, but he danced all the rest of the time with Tiptoe, who had stopped sneezing and felt quite warm with the lamb's tail round her neck.

"I'll see you home," said Bun, after the party. "You can wear the fur all the way to the foxglove bed, and when you're nice and warm at home, you can give me the tail to take back to the baby lamb, who lent it to me. I lost my own tail."

"How sad for you!" said Tiptoe. "But what a good thing for me, because if you hadn't lost your own tail you wouldn't have been able to lend me this fur, and I should have had to go home early! Tomorrow I'll have a good hunt for your own tail, Bun. Now, goodnight, and thank you for your kindness."

Bun said goodnight and ran home very happy. He told all the toys what had happened and the baby lamb was very pleased when he heard how useful his tail had been. The teddy bear pinned it on to his back again, and then all the toys settled themselves to sleep.

Next evening there came a tapping at the playroom window and who should it be but Tiptoe!

"Bun!" she called. "Bun! Come quickly! I've found your tail!"

Bun ran to the window and opened it. There was Tiptoe, and in her hand was Bun's own little short tail.

"Where did you find it?" he asked, in delight.

"A worm had pulled it down into his hole," said Tiptoe. "I took it away from him and washed it. Now it is dry and clean, and if you come with me I'll sew it on so tightly for you that you will never lose it again."

So Bun went to the foxglove bed with Tiptoe and she sewed his tail on for him again with a hundred stitches so that it was very firm indeed.

"You are the dearest elf I ever saw!" said Bun. "I do wish you would marry me, Tiptoe. We could live in the dolls' house, and be very happy together."

"Ooh, let's!" said Tiptoe, and she flung her arms round Bun and hugged him. He had never been so happy in all his life.

They moved into the dolls' house, and, oh, what a merry time they had! They gave parties every night, and Tiptoe learnt to cook lovely cakes on the little tin stove in the kitchen. And they *always* ask the baby lamb to their parties, because if it hadn't been for his long woolly tail Bun and Tiptoe would never have got married!

Paddy the puppy

Alan was staying with his Auntie Betty and his cousin Jenny. He liked it very much except that Auntie Betty was much stricter than his own mother!

She made him wipe his feet properly and hang up his things as soon as he took them off. "If you throw them down on the floor again you won't have any cake for tea!" she told him – and when he forgot, she kept her word and he *didn't* have cake for tea! He sulked, and Cousin Jenny laughed at him.

There was a lovely big garden to play in, and Jenny had a little bicycle and a tricycle too, so they had some fine racing. There was a swing to swing on and a sandpit to play in, so there was always plenty to do.

"Remember to bring in your toys when you come in!" Auntie Betty said. Jenny always remembered and Alan always forgot! Then out he had to go and collect them all.

"Remember to shut the gate when

you go out in case the puppy runs out and gets run over," said Auntie Betty, each morning. And again, Jenny always remembered, and Alan always forgot!

Auntie Betty was cross then. "Don't you *like* the puppy, Alan?" she would say. "Don't you care enough for the little thing to remember to shut the gate? You are unkind!"

"I *do* like him," said Alan. "I love him. He's a darling and I do love the way he wags his tail and comes running to meet me. I *will* remember to shut the gate."

"If anything happens to Paddy because of you, I'll never, never forgive you!" said Cousin Jenny. "You don't even *try* to remember things! I think you must have a very poor sort of brain."

"I *haven't*!" said Alan, at once. "My mother says I'm going to be clever. I've nearly been top at school three times!"

"Well, you're not clever *now!*" said Jenny. "Who left his toys out in the rain yesterday again? Who didn't . . ."

"Be quiet!" said Alan, sulkily. "I tell you I'm going to remember everything from now on!"

Certainly that day he was quite good at remembering all he had been told. He even remembered to shut the door quietly after him instead of slamming it. Auntie Betty was surprised!

"We shall send you back home a different boy!" she said. "Your mother will be pleased!"

Jenny and Alan were sent out next day to buy a collar and a lead for little Paddy the pup.

"He's growing now," said Auntie Betty. "He must learn to wear a collar, and to walk nicely on the lead."

"Can I take him out for a walk and teach him?" said Jenny. "Do let me!"

"Well – you're a very sensible little girl, so perhaps I'll let you!" said her mother.

"Can I take Paddy too?" asked Alan at

once. "I'm sensible as well."

"You're not," said Jenny. "You'd lose Paddy or let him get run over or something! He can't be trusted with Paddy, can he, Mummy?"

"We'll see," said her mother. "Anyway, you go and buy him a collar and lead this morning."

Paddy wasn't very pleased with his new collar, and he didn't like the lead at all! When Jenny put it on him and tried to walk him round the garden, he pulled away from her, and tried to escape.

"Oh, Paddy – you're nearly pulling my arm out!" said Jenny. "Walk to heel, and don't drag in front all the time."

"Let *me* take him," said Alan. "I'm a boy and boys' arms are stronger than girls'! I can soon teach him."

It was true that Alan was very good with Paddy. He was very patient and kind, and soon the puppy began to understand what it was that he was supposed to do.

"There you are!" boasted Alan. "I told you I could soon teach him!"

And then, at that very moment, Paddy gave a sudden jerk at the lead, pulled it out of Alan's hand, and ran to the front gate, where he had just seen a doggy friend pass by. The gate was open and the puppy frisked out into the road. A car hooted suddenly and swerved.

"Oh Paddy! He's out in the road!" cried Jenny and ran to get him. Her mother heard the car's hoot and looked out of the window. She was cross when she saw the puppy in the road.

"Who left that front gate open?" she called. And, of course, as usual it was Alan. He went very red in the face. "I did. I'm so sorry. I just came running in and swung it behind me, thinking it would shut all right," he said.

Jenny was hugging the puppy, glaring at her cousin angrily. "He nearly got run over! All because of you! Do you know what I would have done if he had been hurt? I would have thrown all your toys out of the window, and smashed your engine, and I would have told your mother to fetch you home, and – ”

“That's enough, Jenny,” said her mother. “You may be sure that if Alan does anything really bad *I* will deal with him and take him home, not you! Please do try and keep your temper!”

“I've said I was sorry, Jenny,” said Alan.

“It isn't *enough* to be sorry – always to be sorry, sorry, sorry!” cried Jenny. “Why can't you be sensible? Then you wouldn't *have to be sorry!*”

Alan really did try to remember everything properly for the next two days. He was very good with the puppy too, and taught him a great deal. In fact, Paddy was soon walking beautifully on the lead, his nose just touching Alan's heels as he padded along.

“I can take Paddy for a walk, Mummy says,” said Jenny next day. “Not with you. Only by myself.”

"Oh, well, can *I* take him for a walk too, by *myself*?" said Alan. "Auntie, can I?"

"Yes," said his Aunt. "Jenny can take him this morning and you can take him this afternoon."

Jenny took Paddy off proudly, the lead fastened to his nice new collar. When she came back she told her mother that Paddy hadn't *really* been very good.

"He kept wanting to talk to all the other dogs he met," she said. "And sometimes I had to *drag* him away, and that's bad for his neck."

"You could have carried him then," said Alan. "That's what *I* shall do if I have any bother with him this afternoon. But I think he'll be very good with me."

Alan set out with Paddy after dinner. The little dog was delighted to have another walk. He trotted off at Alan's heels, as good as gold.

Alan talked to him all the way and

Paddy listened. "When you are with two-legged people, you don't stop and talk to *four*-legged creatures," Alan explained to him. "That's bad manners. But if *I* stop and talk, you just sit down politely and wait."

Paddy listened and behaved very well indeed. Then he suddenly pricked up his ears, and so did Alan. "Drums! Trumpets! There's a band coming!" he said. "I'll just tie you to this railing, Paddy, and go and stand at the kerb and watch. Sit there, like a good dog!"

Alan ran to the kerb to see the band pass. Rum-tiddy-rum, BOOM-BOOM-BOOM, tan-tan-tan-tara, BOOM! It was a wonderful band, and not only the soldiers were marching in time, but all the passers-by too! Some children came along, marching in a row, and called to Alan.

"Come on – this is fun!"

Alan joined in, and marched with the others, left-right, left-right, boom-diddy-boom, diddy-diddy-boom, boom, BOOM!

He went all the way with the soldiers till they came to their camp and went in through the gate. Then he turned to go home.

But before he had gone very far he remembered something. "Oh – PADDY! I left him tied up. Goodness me – I forgot all about him. Poor little puppy!"

He raced back to the railings to untie the puppy – but to his horror Paddy was gone. Alan stood and stared and then he looked up and down the road. Somebody must have stolen Paddy! He couldn't have got free by himself!

He ran to a woman standing outside a greengrocer's shop, serving her customers. "Oh please – did you see anyone take a puppy away a few minutes ago? He was tied to those railings."

"A puppy? Yes, I heard him whining," said the woman. "And when I looked

round I saw a girl taking his lead from the railing-spike, and leading him away."

"Oh! The wicked girl!" cried Alan. "What was she like? I'll go and tell a policeman!"

"Well – she seemed quite ordinary," said the woman, surprised. "She had on a blue dress with yellow stripes and a blue hat with yellow flowers, and sandals. That's all I remember."

Alan saw a policeman standing at a nearby corner and ran to him. "Please!" he said. "Someone's stolen my puppy. I left him over there for a minute – and a girl in a blue dress with yellow stripes took him away."

"Now, don't you upset yourself," said the policeman, opening his notebook. "Give me your name and address, and the dog's name – and I'll soon make enquiries. Don't you worry!"

Alan felt dreadful. How could he have forgotten little Paddy? Jenny was right, he must have a poor sort of brain.

He loved Paddy. He couldn't bear to think anything had happened to him. Whatever would Jenny say – and Auntie Betty?

"Jenny said she'd throw all my things out of the window!" he remembered. "She said she'd tell my mother and I'd be sent home. How can I go and say I've lost Paddy? I daren't. I simply daren't!"

He decided to go back to his aunt's, slip in at the back door, and go up to pack his things. He would go home to his mother and tell her what a failure he was – he had even lost the puppy he loved! He wouldn't tell Jenny and his aunt what had happened – he wouldn't even see them.

He ran back to the house and slipped in at the back door. No one was about. He went upstairs, found all his toys and clothes and packed them into his bag. Then he crept downstairs, meaning to catch the bus.

And *just* as he tried to slip out of the back door, who should come in but his aunt! How surprised she was to see Alan stealing out with his suitcase!

"Why – whatever are you doing? Where are you going?" she said. And then Alan burst into tears, though he knew it was a babyish thing to do.

"I lost Paddy!" he wailed. "I tied him to a railing and followed a band, and forgot him. And when I got back he wasn't there. A girl came and stole him!"

"Oh, Alan!" said his aunt.

"I told a policeman!" said Alan, wiping his eyes. "I hope he'll put that girl into prison. She's wicked. But I'm wicked too, to forget Paddy."

Suddenly there came a knock at the front door. Auntie Betty went to open it. Outside stood the policeman – and with him were Jenny – and Paddy! A most excited Paddy who flung himself on Alan at once and licked him all over.

"Why – what's this!" said Auntie Betty.

"Mother, this policeman stopped me and said Paddy wasn't mine!" cried Jenny. "I suddenly saw him tied up to a railing all by himself, and he was whining so loudly that I couldn't bear it. Alan wasn't anywhere about – so I guessed he had forgotten Paddy and I untied him and took him shopping with me."

"Er – well – it seems that a bit of a mistake has been made," said the policeman, smiling. "Ah, there's the boy who reported to me that the dog was stolen – stolen by a girl in a blue dress with yellow stripes, he said – so, of course, when I saw this young lady dressed like that, *and* with a dog, well, I had to find out what was happening!"

"You'd better take that boy to prison!" said Jenny, pointing at poor Alan. "He's a bad, wicked boy!"

"Don't be silly, Jenny," said her mother. She thanked the policeman, then said goodbye to him and shut the front door. "Look – Alan is so upset about everything that he has packed his bag and wants to go home. Shall we let him?"

Jenny stared at Alan's red eyes, and watched Paddy trying to comfort him. "I shan't ever forget things again – not after this," said Alan, in a low voice, stroking Paddy's soft head. "If you could just trust me once more . . ."

"All right," said Jenny. "I'll forgive you – but only because Paddy does, see? I don't *really* want you to go home."

So Alan unpacked his bag again and stayed. "You've taught me a lesson, Paddy," he told the puppy. "I've taught *you* plenty of things – and you learnt them well. Now you've taught *me* something, and I'll learn that well too. Do you understand?"

"Wuff!" said Paddy. Yes – of *course* he understood!

The little thimble-plant

Natalie was very good at sewing. "It's in the family!" her mother told her. "Your great-granny embroidered so beautifully that the Queen of England bought some of her work. And you know how well your granny sews."

"Yes – and so do you, Mummy!" said Natalie. "I'm sure no one can make dresses as well as you can!"

Natalie had a beautiful silver thimble. Her great-granny had used it, and her granny had given it to Natalie when she saw that her little granddaughter was going to sew beautifully.

"Here you are," she said. "My mother used it when she embroidered the tablecloth that the Queen bought. You shall have it. She always said that it had magic in it, because she never sewed so well as when she wore that little thimble!"

Natalie always used the silver thimble. It fitted her middle finger exactly, and shone brightly as she pushed the needle in and out of her work. She often wondered if there really *was* magic in it!

Natalie was fond of gardening as well as sewing. She embroidered flowers on cushions, and she loved to copy her own flowers with her needle and coloured cottons. She had the prettiest little garden, full of candytuft, poppies, marigolds and roses.

"You must go in for the flower show this year," her mother said. "Do you know what the prize in the children's section is, Natalie? It's a work-basket! You need a new one, a nice big one. Wouldn't it be lovely if you could win the prize and take home a big new work-basket!"

"Oh, *yes*," said Natalie, delighted. "I'll grow some lovely flowers in my garden and take them to the show. Is the work-basket to be awarded for any special flowers, Mummy?"

"It's for the prettiest and most unusual plant that is flowering in a pot," said her mother. "You could put one of your garden plants into a pot and show that. You have one or two really unusual poppies. Those double red ones with pink stripes are the prettiest I have ever seen. You would be sure to win a prize with those."

Natalie took her sewing into the garden and sat down by her little garden. She looked at it as she sewed. As Mummy said, those red poppies striped curiously with pink might win a prize.

"It really would be fun to bring home that work-basket," said Natalie to herself. "Now, I'll just finish this bit of sewing, then I'll water my garden. It looks very dry."

She finished her sewing, left it on the grass and went to water her garden. The thirsty earth drank up the water thankfully. Natalie pulled up a few weeds, then gathered up her sewing things and went indoors.

But that evening, when she was showing her mother her sewing, she missed her little silver thimble! "Oh dear – where is it?" she said, hunting in her sewing-bag. "Oh, Mummy, I must have left it out on the grass. I'll have to go and look for it. It's still light."

So out she went. But although she hunted through every blade of grass by her garden she couldn't find her silver thimble. She went back to the house, upset.

"It's gone," she said. "Mummy, could anyone have taken it? Nobody comes into the garden, do they? I'm sure I left it down by my garden. But it isn't there now."

Mummy went to look too, and then they turned out the sewing-bag again.

They hunted all over the floor, and down the garden path. But the silver thimble didn't turn up. Natalie was worried.

"Oh, Mummy, I'm sure that was my lucky thimble. I do hope my good luck won't go now I've lost Granny's magic thimble. She always said it had magic in it. I'm sure it had, too. I could always do my best sewing when I was wearing that."

Well, it was a very strange thing, but it did seem as if Natalie's good luck disappeared with her silver thimble. First she fell off her bicycle and hurt her right hand so that she couldn't sew for a week. Then the dog got hold of the new cushion cover she was making for her mother and bit a hole in it. Then she lost one of her school books and got a scolding.

"If only I could find my silver thimble, I'm sure I'd be lucky again," she told her mother.

"Oh, nonsense," said Mummy. "It's

nothing to do with your thimble. Everyone has bad luck at times. I expect yours has finished now. You'll get a bit of good luck instead!"

But her mother was wrong. Three days before the flower show, just when Natalie's garden was looking really beautiful, two sheep wandered in at the back gate and ran all over the lawns and beds. One found its way into Natalie's garden and ate almost every plant in it!

Natalie ran crying to her mother. "Mummy! There's more bad luck! Those sheep, look – one has eaten nearly everything in my garden. My beautiful poppies – I can't possibly enter them for the flower show now. I haven't a chance now of winning that lovely work-basket!"

Mummy was very sad for her. She shook her head when she saw the spoilt garden. The sheep had been chased back to their field – but oh, what a lot of damage they had done! What a pity to spoil all Natalie's lovely flowers!

"Poor Natalie," said Mummy. "Never mind, darling. Nasty things do happen. You just have to make up your mind not to be upset too much. I've always noticed that if you make the best of bad things, something good comes along sooner or later!"

Natalie was very sad. She took her sewing down by her poor spoilt garden and began to embroider poppies on a new cushion-cover. "And if the dog gets this one I really will shout at him!" she thought. "Oh dear – I've got to use this horrid little pink thimble instead of my own lovely silver one. *Where* did it go, I wonder? Is somebody else wearing it now?"

A little robin hopped down beside her to watch her. Natalie called him *her* robin because he always came to watch when she gardened. She spoke to him and he cocked his head on one side, listening.

"I'm sad because my luck has

disappeared with my little silver thimble," she told him. "I did love it so. Robin, *you* haven't seen it, have you? Do you know who has got it? Did it go down a worm-hole – and is the worm using it for a hat?"

That idea made her laugh. The robin listened, and then gave a sudden little trill and flew into the nearby hedge. She heard him singing loudly, almost as if he were telling somebody something. Natalie wished she could understand what he was singing.

And then a most surprising thing happened. Out from the tangle of weeds in the hedge peeped a small face with bright green eyes, and a very long beard. The face wore a pointed hat on its head, and it looked rather worried.

Natalie stared in surprise. Was it a doll? No, it couldn't be – the face was too small. Besides, it moved. It smiled! And then the face moved forward and a whole body appeared, as somebody came through the weeds.

It was a brownie – such a small brownie that Natalie thought he could live in her doll's house with ease. He came right up to her, the robin fluttering behind.

"You're Natalie, aren't you?" said the brownie, his long beard waving round him in the breeze. "The robin told me. And he said you've lost your silver thimble and you're very upset."

"Yes. I loved it," said Natalie. "Do you know where it is? And are you a brownie? I've seen pictures of brownies in my books, but I never thought that one lived just under my hedge!"

"Children aren't as kind to little creatures as they should be," said the brownie. "So we hide away now. But we're always about. The robin told me you were kind, so I'm not afraid to come and speak to you. And I'm really very, very sorry – but I'm afraid *I've* got your thimble. At least, I think it must be what you call a thimble, though I've never used one myself."

"But why did you take it?" asked Natalie gently, afraid of scaring him.

"I found it halfway down a worm-hole," said the brownie. "I heard the worm complaining because he couldn't get out. It was stopping up his way, you see. So I dragged it out and took it home. I didn't know it belonged to you."

"What did you do with it?" asked Natalie, feeling really excited.

"Well, to tell the truth, I thought it was a plant pot," said the brownie. "Silly of me – but I honestly thought it was. So I planted a seed in it to grow and stood it on a little wooden stand on my window-sill. I'll let you have it back at once, of course."

"Oh, please do!" said Natalie, delighted. "I don't mind your having had it for a plant pot at all – if only you'll give it back to me now. I'll give you this little *pink* thimble if you like, for a plant pot."

"Now that's *very* kind of you," said the brownie, and darted off at once.

He came back with Natalie's silver thimble. He carried it upside down, of course, fitted into its stand because to him it was a pot. In it grew a tiny plant with pretty, feathery leaves.

"What have you planted in my thimble?" asked Natalie.

"It's a wing-flower," said the brownie. "Its flowers are just like fairy-wings, you know, in fact, some fairies cut them off and use them for a spare pair. They only need a spell in them to make them fly."

Natalie looked down at the tiny plant in wonder. It had a nice fat bud at the top! Would it flower into tiny fairy-wings? Oh, how wonderful!

"Thank you. I shan't take out this magic little plant till it dies," said Natalie. "Fancy, it's so small that it grows in a thimble! I shall wait and see if it flowers into wings. Look, here is my pink thimble for you. Come and talk to me again sometime. I'll send the robin to call you when I am here all alone."

"I'd like that," said the green-eyed fellow, and nodded his head. "Thank you for the pink thimble. *I* think it's prettier than the other. Goodbye!"

Natalie took the thimble-plant to her mother. How marvellous! What a wonderful thing to happen!

Mummy could really hardly believe it. She looked closely at the tiny plant. "I have *never* seen one like it before," she said. "Oh, Natalie, you ought to show it at the flower show! It's quite perfect. It should be in flower then, too!"

Well, on the day of the flower show the little thimble-plant burst into flower – and to Natalie's great delight the flower was in the shape of fairy-wings, two dainty blue and silver wings, quivering on the stalk.

"It *is* a wing-flower," said Natalie. "Oh, Mummy, if only I was small enough to fly with them! When the flower dies I'll cut off the wings and fasten them to a little dolls' house doll – *she* might fly with them at night!"

She took the thimble-plant to the show. Everyone exclaimed in wonder when they saw such a strange little plant, with tiny wings quivering at the top of the stalk.

"Wonderful! Marvellous! Where did you get it from?"

Natalie whispered her tale to the children, but she didn't think the grown-ups would believe her, so she didn't say anything to them. The children crowded round the thimble-plant, holding their breath in case they damaged the fairy-wings growing at the top.

Well, of course, you can guess who got the prize. Natalie! She would have got the prize for her poppies, if she had shown them, so she really only got what she deserved. But how pleased she was! Mummy carried the big work-basket home for her, and Natalie carefully carried the strange little plant growing from her silver thimble.

She cut off the wings when the flower

seemed dead, though they were still exactly like proper little wings. And, at the foot of the flower, was a tiny ball of seeds – seeds so fine that they seemed almost like powder.

I wish Natalie would give me one. I *would* so love to grow a wing-flower in a silver thimble, wouldn't you?

The little brownies' race

"Now come along, come along, come along!" shouted Old Man Smarty. "Where are you, Shuffle, Trot and Merry? I've some goods here ready for you to take to my house!"

Shuffle, Trot and Merry, the three little brownies, were playing a game of marbles in a corner of the market. Shuffle groaned. "Blow! Now we must take his sacks on our backs and walk for miles to his house. I'm tired of it! Why doesn't he give us horses to ride?"

"Because we're cheaper than horses," said Trot. "Come along."

The three little fellows went along to where Old Man Smarty was standing by three big sacks.

"Oh – so there you are, you lazy lot!" he said. "Now see – I've bought all these things at the market, and I want them taken to my house as fast as possible, because Lord High-Up is sending for them tonight, and will pay me a good price."

"It's too hot to walk fast with big sacks like those!" said Shuffle.

"We shan't get there before midnight," said Trot, gloomily.

"Well – I'll do my best," said Merry.

"I'll give a gold piece to the one who gets to my house first," said Old Man Smarty. "There's generosity for you!"

Trot, Shuffle and Merry pricked up their ears at that! A gold piece! That was riches to them.

Sly old Shuffle went over to the sacks at once, and quickly felt them all. Ooh – what a heavy one – and the second was heavy too – but the third one felt as light as a feather! That was the one for him!

"I shall hardly know I've a sack on my

back!" he thought. "I shall easily be the first one at the master's house, and I shall get the gold piece before either of them is in sight! Oho – I'm clever, I am!"

He shuffled off with the very light sack on his back. Then Trot went over to the two sacks left, and wondered what was in them. He stuck a finger into one – it was full of something round and hard – potatoes, perhaps? He stuck a finger into the other and felt something loose and soft – what was it – flour – salt – sugar? He pulled out his finger and sucked it.

"Ah – *sugar*!" he said. "That's fine! I can cut a tiny hole in the sack and wet my finger and dip it into the sugar all the time I'm walking along. What a treat!"

So Trot took the second sack and set off to catch up with Shuffle. Merry whistled a jolly tune and went to the sack that was left. He made a face as he lifted it on to his back. "It's heavy – full of potatoes, I think – and the sellers haven't cleaned the mud off them, either, and that makes them twice as heavy. Well – here goes – I must catch up Shuffle and Trot before they get too far, or I'll not win that gold piece!"

But it was difficult to catch up with Shuffle, even though he was not the fastest walker as a rule – because his sack was so very, very light. Shuffle had no idea what was inside, and he didn't care. He was delighted to have picked such a light load!

"That gold piece is as good as in my pocket!" he thought to himself. "Instead of being last today I shall be first! And will I share that gold piece with the others? No, certainly not! They don't deserve it – I'm the sharpest of the lot!"

Trot was having quite a good time with his sack. He made a hole in it and as he trotted along he kept putting in his finger, getting it covered in sugar, and then licking it off. What a joke, he thought – he was lightening his load and having a feast at the same time!

Merry walked fast, but his load was really very heavy – and then he had the bad luck to stub his toe on a big stone, and that made him limp!

"Just my luck!" he groaned. "I always seem to get the heaviest load and to be last for some reason or other. Look at Shuffle now – he must have picked the lightest sack of the lot – and judging by the way Trot is poking his finger in and out of that sack, it's full of something nice to eat. Oh, my toe! I'll never get that gold piece. I can't walk fast with a sore toe!"

So Merry fell behind, but all the same he whistled a merry tune and had a joke for anyone he met.

Now very soon clouds began to cover the sun, and a wind blew up and made the trees sway to and fro. Then Merry felt a drop of rain on his face and he sighed.

"Now it's going to pour with rain and I shall get soaked. I'd better give up all hope of getting that gold piece!"

The rain began to pelt down, stinging the faces of the three little fellows with their sacks. Shuffle was a great way ahead of the others, and he grinned as he looked round and saw how distant Trot was. As for Merry, he was almost out of sight, he was so far behind.

But, as the rain poured down, queer things began to happen! First of all, Shuffle's sack became gradually heavier. He didn't notice it at first, and then he began to wonder.

"*Is* my sack getting heavy, or am I just imagining it?" he thought. He humped it over his shoulder and groaned. "My word, it feels twice as heavy! Whatever can be inside?"

He walked a little further and then felt that he must have a rest, for the sack was so terribly heavy. He set it down and undid the rope that tied the neck. He put in his hand and felt something soft and squashy. What could it be? The squashy thing was very wet indeed for the rain had penetrated right into the sack. Shuffle pulled it out and looked at it.

It was a sponge! A *sponge*! "No wonder the sack felt so light when the sponges were dry!" said Shuffle, in dismay. "Now they're soaked with rain water and as heavy as can be! What can I do?"

He took all the sponges out of the sack and squeezed them dry, and then began to put them back into the sack again. "But what's the use of that?" he groaned. "The rain is as heavy as ever, and the sponges will soon be full of water again!"

Trot came up and grinned. "Hello, Shuffle – so your load was sponges, was it? It serves you right for picking the lightest load as usual. Now you've got the heaviest!"

"What's in yours?" called Shuffle, annoyed, but Trot didn't stop. No, he saw a chance of winning that gold piece now. He was going quite fast. Also, his sack felt lighter!

In fact, it soon felt so light that Trot stopped in surprise. "What's happening to my sack?" he thought. "It really does feel remarkably light!"

He set it down to see – and, to his horror, he found that the sugar was all melting in the rain! The raindrops had soaked through the sack and the sugar was dissolving into sweetened water – and dripping fast out of the bottom of the sack!

"I ought to get under cover, or it will all be melted away," thought Trot, in dismay. "Why wasn't I sensible enough to remember that sugar melts? I *knew* it was sugar all right! Well, I've outpaced old Shuffle – but if I wait till the rain stops Merry will be sure to catch me up and pass me, and I shan't get that gold piece."

So on he went in the pouring rain, while the sugar in his sack melted faster than ever. But at least he was now in the lead!

As for Merry he still whistled in the

pouring rain, for he was a light-hearted fellow. The rain ran into his sack, down among the potatoes and soon muddy water was dripping out at the bottom. Merry laughed.

"You're washing all the dirty potatoes for me!" he said to the rain clouds above. "Hello – there's Shuffle in front of me – he's very slow today!"

He soon passed Shuffle, who groaned loudly as Merry passed him. "My load is sponges!" he shouted. "And they're four times as heavy as they were now that they're soaked with rain."

"Serves you right!" said Merry. "You picked the lightest sack so that you could win that gold piece!"

The three went on through the rain, and at last came one by one to Old Man Smarty's big house. Trot went round to the back door first of all and set down his sack on the ground.

"Ha!" said the big cook, "so you've brought something for the master, have you? Well, wait till he calls you in to see him. I'll tell him you were the first."

The next was Merry with his sack of potatoes. The cook peered at them and smiled. "Well I never – the potatoes are all washed clean for me! That's a good mark for you, Merry. Wait here till the master sends for you."

Last of all came poor Shuffle, very weary with carrying such a wet and heavy load. He set his sack down and water ran all over the floor.

"Now pick up that sack and stand it outside!" said the cook. "My floor's in enough mess already without you making it a running river. What in the world have you got in that sack?"

But Shuffle was too tired to answer. The cook gave them all some food and drink and they sat back and waited to take their sacks to the master.

The call came at last, and the cook took them in to Old Man Smarty.

"Here's the first one – he came before the others," she said, pushing Trot forward. His sack looked limp, wet and empty. Old Man Smarty glared at it.

"What's this? It should be full of sugar! Where's the sugar, Trot? Have you sold it to someone on the way?"

"No, sir. It was the rain that melted it," said Trot. "I was first here, sir. Can I have my gold piece?"

"Bah!" said Old Man Smarty. "Why didn't you get under cover and save my expensive sugar?" Then he turned to Shuffle. "Shuffle, you were third, so you're out of it. Take that disgusting, dripping sack out of the room. Merry, what about you?"

"Sir, he's brought potatoes — and they're all washed clean!" said the cook, eagerly, for she liked Merry. "He *deserves* the gold piece, even though he wasn't the first here!"

"*I* was first!" said Trot. "*I* won the gold. Give it to me, Old Man Smarty!"

"Very well — but *you* must pay me *two* gold pieces for all the sugar you've lost out of my sack," said Old Man Smarty. "That's what it cost me! So if I give you one gold piece, you have to give me two."

"All right. I won't claim it," said Trot, sulkily. "I should have got the sack under cover." He stamped out of the room in a rage. Only Merry was left.

"You weren't the first," said Old Man Smarty. "But you certainly delivered my goods in a better condition than when I bought them — so I shall award the gold piece for that."

He tossed a shining coin to the delighted Merry, who went off to the kitchen with his sack of potatoes. What sulks and grumbles met him from Shuffle and Trot! He clapped them on the shoulder. "Cheer up — we'll go and spend my gold piece together. What's good luck for but to be shared!"

They all went out arm in arm and the cook stared after them. "You deserve your good luck, Merry!" she called. "And what's more, you'll always get it — a merry face and a generous heart are the luckiest things in the world!"

Bom and the drum

I expect you've heard of Bom, the little toy drummer who goes about the world beating his drum and looking for adventures.

Well, one day he went marching through the woods, beating his big drum and wishing he had some money in his pocket to buy some dinner, because he was very hungry.

Just as he passed under a hazel tree, the wind blew – and something dropped on his head and fell to the ground.

"A nut!" said Bom, pleased. "A hazel nut! Good, I'll pick some and eat them – not a very good dinner, but I am so very hungry."

So he took one of his drumsticks and

beat some ripe hazel nuts down from the tree, each in its little green-brown coat. He took off his drum and sat down to eat them. He had nothing but his teeth to crack them with, so it was lucky for him that they were strong.

He hadn't eaten more than three nuts when he heard a noise overhead. He looked up. A small red squirrel sat on a branch in the hazel tree, stamping his front feet and grumbling to himself.

"My nuts! There are hardly any left on my own special tree. Where have they gone?"

"Hello, Squirrel," said Bom, surprised. "*I've* been picking the nuts. But there are plenty, so do come down and share them."

Down scampered the squirrel and took some of the nuts. "You're kind," he said. "Thank you. It isn't really *my* tree, it's just one I specially like." He cracked the shells easily with his sharp teeth to get at the sweet kernel inside. "Shall I crack some for you?" he offered. "My teeth are made for cracking nuts, and yours aren't. You might break them!"

"Thank you," said Bom, and soon the little red squirrel was cracking a whole pile of nuts for Bom to eat.

"It's very kind of you," said Bom. "Can I do anything in return?"

"Oh, no – you gave me some of your nuts to eat, didn't you!" said the squirrel. "But all the same – there *is* one thing I'd like to do."

"What?" asked Bom.

"Well, could I just leap about on that drum of yours, and drum a tune with my four feet?" asked the squirrel. "It would make me feel very grand, you know."

Bom laughed. "Yes, of course you can, you funny little creature."

The red squirrel jumped on the drum in delight, and beat it with his four quick little feet.

Bommy-bommy-bom-bom-bom, diddy-diddy-diddy-bom-bom, boom, boom, BOOM!

Two small rabbits came out of their holes, and a robin flew down to listen. Then more squirrels came and sat round watching and listening.

"He's drumming – isn't he clever, he's drumming!" they said to one another, and the squirrel on the drum felt very proud indeed.

Then suddenly someone called out. "Hist! Here comes a strange fellow through the wood!"

And in a trice all the squirrels and rabbits vanished, and the robin flew away, too.

Bom wondered who was coming. He heard someone whistling, and then the sound of feet walking through the dry bracken. Who was it?

"Gracious – it's a clown!" said Bom, in surprise. "He must have come from that circus I passed this morning. I don't much like the look of him."

"Hello!" said the clown, stopping beside Bom. "I heard the noise of drumming as I came through the wood.

I say, that's a fine drum of yours."

"Yes. It's certainly a big one," said Bom, eating a nut.

"You seem very hungry," said the clown.

"I am," said Bom. "I've had nothing to eat but these nuts all day. I haven't a single penny to buy anything."

"I'll give you ten pence if you let me beat your drum for a while," said the clown, tapping his fingers on the drum, making it go *bom-diddy-bom* very quietly indeed.

"Ten pence! Well, that would buy me a sandwich in the next village," said Bom, cheering up. "Bang the drum as much as you like!"

The clown beat the drum loudly. *Bom-bom-bom-diddy-bom-bom-bom!*

"This is fine," he said. "You must feel very grand going along the roads beating a drum like this. Everyone must come running out to see you."

"Oh, yes, they do," said Bom, proudly.

"If I give you another ten pence would

you let me wear your drum for a little while, and march up and down with it, banging it with your two drumsticks?" asked the clown.

"Well, so long as you don't want to go on too long," said Bom. "I'm longing to go and buy something to eat!"

"All right. Here's another ten pence," said the clown, pleased, and threw Bom the coin. Then he put on the drum, took up the drumsticks and began to march up and down, banging loudly. "Oh, I do feel grand!" he said. "I wish everyone at my circus could see me! *Bom-bom-bom!*"

He walked down the path to a tree and then came back, beating the drum. Then he turned and marched up to the tree again – but this time he didn't come back. He went on marching!

Bom could hear the beating of his drum, although now he couldn't see the clown.

"Hey – come back!" he shouted. But

the clown *didn't* come back. And then, oh dear, Bom couldn't hear the drumming any more. He stood up at once and ran down the path.

"Hey, Clown! Where are you? Bring back my drum!"

But the clown was nowhere to be seen. He had gone quickly through the wood, beating the drum; then suddenly he had stopped banging it, and stood listening. Good – he was quite alone!

"I'll hide the drum under this bush, then go to that cave over there and hide till Bom has given up trying to find me," he said. "Then I'll take the drum for my own." So he pushed the big drum under the bush and ran to hide in the cave.

Nobody saw him except the little red squirrel who had shared Bom's nuts with him. He had scampered overhead in the trees, watching where the clown went. He saw him push the drum under the bush, and then go off to the cave.

"He means to take the drum when Bom has stopped looking for him," thought the little squirrel. "Poor Bom, what a shame. I'll go and fetch my friends."

So he bounded off to get help.

Not long afterwards Bom came along shouting for the clown. But he couldn't see him anywhere, of course, because he was down in the dark cave; nor did he see his drum under the bush as he rushed quickly by.

As soon as Bom was gone, the clown crept out of his cave. Now, where was the bush in which he had hidden that drum? Goodness, he had forgotten!

But the little squirrel hadn't forgotten. He had brought his friends to the bush, and they were trying to pull out the big drum. But they were not strong enough to move it.

"Look out – the clown's coming out of his cave," said a small squirrel, suddenly. "Whatever shall we do? Oh, look, there's a little door in the side of the drum. Let's all jump inside it, shall we – then if the clown does find the

drum, it will be too heavy for him to move – there'll be so many of us inside!"

So one by one they slipped through the little door in the drum, and shut it behind them. They were all scrabbling about inside, packed as closely as could be.

"Ah, here's the bush where I hid the drum," said the clown coming up, and he gave the drum a tug to get it out. "My word, it feels terribly heavy. What's happened to it?"

At last he got it out from under the bush – but he couldn't lift it to put it on and beat it. No, it was far too heavy. He just managed to roll it a little way and then he grew frightened, because so many strange noises came from inside the drum. He didn't know there was a little door that opened in the side.

The squirrels fell about in the drum as the clown rolled it along, and they squeaked and squawked loudly.

The clown was frightened. "The

drum's alive! It's yelling at me! It's made itself too heavy to move," he cried. "Go away, Drum, I'm scared of you!"

He turned and ran away at top speed. As soon as the squirrels in the drum heard him running they opened the little door and sprang out. "He's gone! Look at him running!" they cried, pointing after the clown. "Now we must find Bom."

"He went down that path over there," said the smallest squirrel. "Let's take the drum and go after him."

"But we're too small to carry a big drum like this," said another squirrel.

"Well, look – let's bowl it along like a great hoop," said the smallest one, taking up a drumstick. "You take the other stick, Brother. Come along – away we go, after Bom!"

And away they went, bowling the big drum along merrily.

"There's Bom, look!" cried the smallest squirrel at last. "Stop bowling! I'll beat the drum, and he'll hear it and come back. Now – *bom-diddy-bom-diddy-bom-bom BOM!*"

As soon as he heard *that* noise, Bom stopped at once, and turned round. "Oh – there's my drum, right away up that path!" he cried. "Hey, Drum, here I am!"

And then to his surprise, the drum rolled towards him, because the squirrels were bowling it along with the drumsticks again.

Bom soon saw that the little squirrels were with it and he laughed to see them.

"Oh, you *are* good friends," he cried. "However did you get my drum back for me? Thank you, thank you! I'll put it on at once, and march down to the village I can see over there. Please, do come with me and help me to spend my ten pences!"

So there they go, Bom beating his drum, and all the little red squirrels proud to be with him – one on his head, two on his shoulders, and one on the drum itself, hopping about happily, and the rest skipping behind.

The bold, bad boys!

D erek and Tom loved to go down and play beside the river. They liked watching the boats go by, and when a steamer sailed along in midstream, making quite big waves break against the banks, they shouted with joy.

"Daddy, can't we have a boat of our own?" begged Derek. "Lots of the boys we know have. Why can't we?"

"For a very good reason," said Daddy. "You can't swim yet! I tried to teach you last summer, but you both cried because the water was cold, and Tom yelled when I held him up and tried to make him do the arm-strokes."

The two boys looked rather ashamed. "If you'd let us have a boat, we promise we will learn to swim this summer," said Derek.

"Oh, no!" said Daddy. "I'll promise you a boat when you have learnt to swim. That's the right way to put it."

The boys went off, rather sulky. "Lots of people who can't swim have boats," said Tom. "How can we have adventures, and go rowing off to find them, if we haven't got a boat. Daddy's mean."

"Never mind," said Derek. "We'll have a good time paddling. We'll call ourselves The Bold, Bad Boys and we'll look for adventures every single day. We'll be pirates and smugglers, and we'll be very bold and daring."

So they were. They became a great nuisance to the moorhens by the river, and the big swans hissed at them as they sailed grandly by. But when the cows came down to stand in the shallow part of the river, The Bold, Bad Boys ran away. They were rather afraid of cows!

Now, one day, when the two boys were sitting by the water, splashing it with their feet, they saw something coming down the river. It wasn't a boat. It wasn't a bird. What could it be?

"It's a barrel! An empty barrel, floating along by itself!" cried Derek. "If only we could get it, Tom. We could play smugglers properly if we had a barrel of our own! We could even hide in it."

They watched the barrel. It came bobbing along – and floated to where a low branch stretched out from the bank over the water. There it caught and stopped.

"Look, look!" cried Derek. "That branch has caught it. Oh, Tom, let's be really bold and crawl out on that branch and get the barrel. I think the water is shallow there, and maybe we could get on the barrel and push it over to the bank."

So, feeling very bold and daring, the two boys crawled along the branch to the barrel. Derek leaned down and caught hold of it.

"Tom, can you get on to the barrel whilst I hold it?" he said. "Quick, in case I have to let go. That's right. Oh, good, you're riding the barrel! Will it take me too, do you think?"

Tom had dropped neatly on to the barrel, and was now riding it astride, grinning happily. Derek dropped down beside him.

Now they were both on the barrel. "Work hard with your feet and we'll get it to the bank," said Derek. But, alas, as soon as they left the tree branch, the barrel, instead of going towards the bank, got caught by the midstream current and swung out into deep water. Then it began floating merrily down the river with the two boys riding it!

Tom screamed. "Derek, Derek! We're out in deep water. We'll drown!"

"Not if we cling to the barrel," said Derek, going rather white. "Hold on, Tom. Don't let go whatever you do. Oh,

gracious, we're going fast!"

"I feel sick, I feel sick," wailed Tom. "I want to be rescued. Ooooooooh!"

Derek was scared, too. He clung to the bobbing barrel and looked round to see if any boat was about. Not one was anywhere to be seen. So on they bobbed and on and on.

Tom was crying.

Then suddenly a fisherman by the river saw them. "Help, help!" cried Derek. "Save us!"

In the greatest astonishment the fisherman ran to a small boat nearby and got into it. With three or four strong pulls at the oars he was soon alongside the barrel. He pulled the boys into the boat. Tom burst into wails.

"We were nearly drowned. Take me home to Mummy."

The fisherman rowed to shore. He found out where the boys lived and took them both back, wet and scared. Daddy came out when he saw them.

"Whatever's the matter?" he said.

"Have you fallen in the river?"

"No, oh no!" wailed Tom. "We saw a barrel floating down and we crawled out on a tree branch to it . . ."

"And got on it, meaning to take it to the bank, and it floated away with us," said Derek.

"I rescued them in time," said the fisherman, winking at Daddy. "Seems to me they're strange boys, not liking an adventure. Most boys are looking out for one every day."

"So do Tom and Derek," said their father. "In fact, I believe they call themselves The Bold, Bad Boys, and half the time they're smugglers and pirates. And when a little adventure like this comes along, they yell and howl and can't bear it! Well, well, well!"

"Why didn't they swim to shore?" asked the fisherman, surprised to hear all this.

"I'm sorry to have to tell you — but both boys are too scared to learn to swim," said Daddy, solemnly. "They want a boat – and yet they can't swim!"

"Well, they had a barrel for a boat, and they didn't seem to like that at all," said the fisherman. "I reckon a boat would be wasted on them, sir."

"Just what I think," said Daddy. "Well, thanks for rescuing them. Maybe one day they will welcome an adventure when they get one, instead of howling about it."

"Thanks for rescuing us, sir," said Derek, his face very red indeed. He felt so ashamed. To think they were the two Bold, Bad Boys, always looking out for an adventure, and now they had behaved like this!

Derek took Tom into the garden into their secret corner. "We're going to learn to swim!" he told Tom fiercely. "Do you hear, Tom? And there's to be no moaning and groaning about it. We're going to make Daddy proud of us for a change!"

Well, the last time I saw Derek and Tom they were in a small, neat boat of their own, rowing out on the river. So I knew they had learnt to swim, and could really look for exciting adventures. Do you know what they have called their boat? Guess! It's called *The Bold, Bad Boys*!

The doll that ran away to sea

Lulu had eleven dolls, and she used to sit them in a row on the playroom table every night before she went to bed. There were two fairy dolls, two baby dolls, one walking doll, one French doll with real eyelashes, two wooden Dutch dolls, two little Japanese dolls — and one sailor doll.

Now the sailor doll was a boy doll, and he didn't like being all day long with fairy dolls, baby dolls and others. He said he would rather be with soldiers or teddy bears. He thought the other dolls were silly.

"I ought to belong to a boy!" he said. "I

don't like living with a lot of sillies like you!"

All the dolls thought him very rude, and they told him so.

"You ought to be glad to live in a playroom like this, with a kind owner

who doesn't pull us to pieces!" said the walking doll.

"I want adventures!" said the sailor doll. "I'd like to have a boat of my own, and go to sea! Oh, how brave I'd be! I'd fight pirates and sharks, I'd be wrecked on an island, and make a boat of my own. You don't know how brave I am!"

"No, we don't," said one of the fairy dolls. "But we know who ran away when a spider came on to the table the other night, though!"

The sailor doll went red, and didn't say any more. But that night he made up his mind to run away and go to sea. He knew that there was a stream at the bottom of the garden, and he had seen a little toy boat there, made of paper.

"I'll go right away from these silly dolls," he thought. "I'll sail away tonight and be a daring sailor!"

So that night, when Lulu had sat all her dolls in a row on the table, with the sailor doll in the middle, he got up and said goodbye.

"I'm going!" he told them. "You are a lot of babies, and a sailor like me wants adventures! Goodbye!"

He slid down the tablecloth and went to the window. He climbed up on a chair, and then got on the window-sill. The window was open at the bottom, and the sailor doll slipped out. He jumped on to the grass below, and hurried off down the garden. The moon was just rising, but the garden was full of shadows. Things looked quite different from the daytime.

"Tvit! Tvit!" a loud voice suddenly cried above him, and he jumped in fright. Then a large thing flew close to his head, and the sailor doll was so frightened that he fell flat to the ground.

"Oh, it's only a doll!" said the big brown owl, in disappointment. "I thought it was a mouse."

"Was that horrid thing an owl?" said the doll to himself, and he got up, feeling rather ashamed of himself. He went on

105

down the path, and then gave a yell.

"Ooh! A snake! A great crawly snake!"

"Don't be silly," said the owl, flying low down. "That's a big worm coming out for a night stroll. What a little coward you are!"

"No, I'm not," said the sailor doll, sticking out his chest. "I'm as brave as can be! I'm not a bit afraid!"

Just as he said that, who should come rushing round the corner of the path but Prickles the hedgehog, hurrying to find some beetles for his supper. He bumped right into the sailor doll, who began to howl with pain.

"Ooh, I've walked into a lot of needles! Ooh, I'm being pricked all over! What is it, what is it?"

"What a noise you make, to be sure!" said the hedgehog. "I'm sorry I ran into you, but really, you should look where you're going, you know."

Prickles ran off, and left the doll rubbing all the places in which he had been pricked. Then the doll stuck out his chest again and went on, making up his mind to be really brave, whatever happened.

He had almost got down to the stream when something ran up to him. The sailor doll thought he was going to be bitten, and turned and ran away, full of fear. He heard the patter of footsteps after him, and he ran faster. But the footsteps came faster still, and then he heard a little squeaky voice.

"Please, Mister, stop a minute! Can you tell me the time?"

It was a tiny mouse! Oh dear, how dreadfully ashamed of himself the sailor doll was. He stopped at once, and pretended that he hadn't really been running away at all.

"I haven't a watch," he said. "But if you listen hard, you will hear the church clock striking soon, and then you will know what time it is."

"Thank you," said the little mouse. "You're not very brave, are you? Ho ho, it was funny to see you run away from me!"

The sailor doll didn't answer. He went straight down to the stream, and looked for the paper boat. It was there, drawn up on the bank, all ready to sail. The doll felt very brave. He pushed it out on the water, and got in. Then he gave a shout!

"Ho!" he cried. "I'm a sailor doll, and I'm running away to sea!"

A big frog popped its head out of the water, and then it swam to the paper boat.

"Take me with you!" it cried. "I'll be your crew!"

It put its head over the side of the paper boat, and the sailor doll was in a terrible fright.

"What a horrid-looking monster!" he said. "Go away! Go away!"

"No, I'm coming with you!" said the frog, and it began to climb into the boat.

"I shall be eaten, I know I shall!"

shouted the sailor doll in fear. The frog climbed right into the boat – but it was too heavy for the little paper vessel, which suddenly began to fill with water.

"Oh, it's sinking, it's sinking!" cried the sailor doll. And sure enough in half a minute the little boat had sunk to the bottom. The frog swam off in disgust, and the sailor doll had to scramble to shore as best he could. He was wet through, cold and frightened. He thought of the warm nursery, and his old friends, the dolls, all sitting in a neat row on the table, chatting to each other through the night. How he wished he was back with them!

"I'll go back home!" said the sailor doll, with tears in his eyes. "I'm not a bit brave. I am much sillier than even the baby dolls! I hate adventures!"

He ran off up the garden path, and climbed in at the window again. He hauled himself up the tablecloth and ran to where the dolls all sat in a row.

How surprised they were to see him!

"Oh, you poor thing, you're wet through!" cried the walking doll. "Let me dry you with a piece of the tablecloth."

"We *are* glad to see you back!" said the two fairy dolls. "Couldn't you find the way to go to sea?"

"No," said the sailor doll. "The way is full of dreadful flying dragons, and snakes, and prickly monsters, and the stream is full of things that climb into boats and sink them. Adventures are horrid. I don't want them any more. I am glad to be home with you again."

"Poor old sailor doll!" said everyone. "Never mind, we'll be nice to you!"

So they all settled down together once more, and the sailor doll never said again that he wanted to go to sea.

And wasn't Lulu astonished to find him so wet the next morning! She *couldn't* think what had happened – and the sailor doll was much too ashamed to tell her!

Pink! Pink!

Hey-Presto, the wizard, had a wonderful cloak. Whenever he swung it round his shoulders he disappeared at once, because it had very powerful magic in it.

The cloak was most useful to the wizard. He wore it whenever he wanted to be invisible, and then he was able to do all kinds of things.

He could slip into other wizards' castles and watch them at their magic work without being seen. He could go into Witch Green-Eyes' cottage and stand unseen beside her as she stirred spells into her big black pot. He could swing his cloak round him when visitors came that he didn't want to bother about. Nobody could see him then!

"A most useful cloak!" said Hey-Presto, whenever he hung it up in his cupboard, and locked the door. "An invaluable cloak! I couldn't do without it. I must never, never let my enemies get it."

One day when he took it out of the cupboard, Miggy, his old servant, saw it.

"Good gracious, Master!" she said. "How *can* you wear that dirty old cloak? What colour is it meant to be? It's so dirty that I can't even tell if it's blue, red or green!"

"It's pink," said the wizard, looking at it. "At least, it's *supposed* to be pink! It *does* look dirty, doesn't it? Well, well – I suppose I've used it for over a hundred years now – no wonder it is dirty!"

"It's smelly, too," said Miggy, wrinkling her nose. "Pooh! It needs washing, Master. Fancy using a thing for over a hundred years and not having it washed. And look at this hole!"

"Dear me, yes," said the wizard, quite alarmed. "It won't do to get big holes in it – bits of me will be seen then, through the holes. Whatever shall I do?"

"I'll wash and mend it," said Miggy, firmly.

"It's too precious," said Hey-Presto, clutching it tightly.

"Now listen," said Miggy, "that cloak smells so dirty that very soon people will know you are near them, even though you're invisible. You let me wash it. I'll be very, very careful."

"All right, Miggy. But when you hang it out to dry, please put up a clothes line in the walled garden and make sure the gate is locked," said Hey-Presto. "If anyone saw this cloak on the line they might steal it!"

"Oh, Master, I'll be as careful of your cloak as if it was made of gold!" said old Miggy, putting it over her arm. "My word – what a horrible smell! It must be *five* hundred years old, not one!"

She went off and got a tub full of

boiling water. In went the magic cloak, and Miggy scrubbed it up and down in the suds.

"Just look at the dirt coming out," said Miggy, in disgust. "Why, there's more dirt than cloak! I'll have to wash it three or four times before it's really clean."

When she had finished washing it, she could hardly believe her eyes! The cloak was pink – the loveliest pink imaginable!

Miggy shook it out and then called her master. "Master, come here! Did you ever see such a lovely colour in your life?"

Hey-Presto looked at his cloak. Why, it didn't seem the same one! "It's the colour of almond blossom!" he said. "It's the colour of wild roses in the hedge! And yes – it's exactly the colour of the sky when it's pink at sunset time!"

"Yes," said Miggy. "Shame on you for wearing it so dirty! I'm going to hang it out to dry and then I'll mend it for you."

"In the walled garden, mind!" called the wizard, anxiously. "Nobody can get in there, nobody at all."

Miggy hurried into the walled garden. She had already put up a washing line there. She went to the door in the wall and locked it carefully, putting the key into her pocket. Now nobody could get into the garden from outside, and the walls were far too high to climb.

She looked at the clouds racing across the sky. "Nice windy day – the cloak will dry quickly!" she thought. "I'll press it tonight and mend it – and I'll see that the master doesn't get it so dirty again. It shan't go for more than twenty years this time before it's washed again."

She pegged the cloak carefully on the line and watched it flapping in the wind. It would soon be dry!

"I'll fetch it about three o'clock," she thought and trotted indoors. She kept an eye on it through the kitchen window, and was pleased to see that it was drying nicely.

At three o'clock she went into the garden to unpeg the cloak – but it wasn't there! The line was empty – and three or four clothes pegs lay scattered on the ground!

Miggy gave a scream that brought Hey-Presto out at once. "MASTER! MASTER! Your cloak's been stolen!"

Hey-Presto came at top speed. He saw the empty washing line and the scattered pegs and he groaned. He ran to the garden door that led out into the lane, but it was locked. No one could have got in that way.

"I kept that cloak under my eye the whole time," sobbed Miggy. "I looked out from the kitchen window almost every minute. Nobody could have got in without my seeing them, nobody! They couldn't get out without being seen either."

"Oh, yes they could," said Hey-Presto, grimly. "All the thief had to do was to swing the cloak round his shoulders and he and the cloak too would be invisible at once. He could go where he liked then – even creep in past you through the kitchen, out into the hall and walk out of the front door. Nobody would see him. What *am* I to do? My wonderful cloak! I MUST get it back!"

"The thief won't always be wearing it, sir, and it's such a bright, glowing pink that it would be very easy to recognize it," said poor Miggy, very upset indeed. "Can't you offer a reward, Master, to anyone – even to any animal or bird – who finds it or brings news of it?"

"Yes. Yes, I'll certainly do that," said Hey-Presto. Immediately he sent out hundreds of little pixie heralds, complete with trumpets, to announce his loss and the reward for finding the cloak.

Everyone was excited. The country was searched from top to bottom. But no news came in. Nobody had ever seen the cloak, hardly anyone had even known of it – so how *could* it have been stolen?

Rabbits searched down burrows. Fish

in the rivers hunted here and there. Owls looked in hollow trees, swallows looked in barns. It was no good – nobody saw anything pink that was big enough to be the cloak.

And then one day a chaffinch flew down to Miggy in great excitement. "Pink!" he called loudly. "PINK-PINK!"

"What do you mean? Have you found the pink cloak?" cried Miggy. "Where is it?"

"Pink-pink-pink!" shouted the little chaffinch, fluffing out his pretty chest. "PINK!"

"I'll come with you," said Miggy, putting on her bonnet. "Lead the way, Chaffinch. I'm sure you think you've found the cloak!"

"Chip-chip-chip-chip, cherry-erry-erry, chippy, HERE-WE-ARE!" sang the chaffinch, flying up into a tall tree just outside the walled garden. And there, caught on a high branch, and wrapped round and round it, was the magic cloak, as pink as ever, but a little dirty.

"Yes! You're right! It *is* the cloak!" cried Miggy. "You clever bird, you VERY clever bird! Wait here till I get a ladder, and don't you DARE to tell anyone else!"

She fetched a long ladder and up and up she went. She unwrapped the cloak from the branch and slipped it round her so that she might use both her hands to climb down the ladder again. At once, to the chaffinch's astonishment, she vanished and the cloak vanished, too!

"Pink!" he called anxiously. Miggy's voice answered him from the ladder.

"It's all right. I'm still here, climbing down the ladder. Wearing the cloak is the easiest way for me to carry it!"

She ran to the wizard, taking the cloak off just as she got to him. "Master! It's found! Here it is!"

"Where was it?" asked Hey-Presto, startled and delighted.

"Caught up in a tree not far from the walled garden!" said Miggy. "Nobody stole it! The strong wind must have blown it off the line straight up into the tree, and wrapped it round a branch – and there it's been ever since!"

"But who found it?" asked Hey-Presto, looking to see if the cloak was damaged.

"The chaffinch who nests in that tree," said Miggy. "He came and told me. He was so excited he could only say, 'Pink! Pink!' But I guessed what he meant, of course."

"Then he must have the reward," said Hey-Presto. "Call him here, the clever bird."

The chaffinch came. He flew in at the window, calling, "Pink! Pink!"

"There! He can't say anything but that at the moment," said Miggy. "He's been shouting out the news to everyone – he's so proud of himself!"

"Chaffinch, you have earned the reward," said Hey-Presto, and the little bird flew on to his shoulder. "You may have a sack of gold – a box of spells – or anything else you can think of."

The chaffinch whispered a little song into the wizard's ear. Hey-Presto laughed.

"What does he want for a reward?" asked Miggy.

"Nothing! He says money is no use to him – and he's frightened of spells – and as he has a nest of his own, with a dear little wife and four beautiful nestlings, he has got everything he can possibly want," said the wizard. "He just wants to know if he can go on telling everyone that he found my pink cloak – he's so very, very proud of that."

"Well, let him," said Miggy. "It's a reward that won't cost you a penny – and he'll be glad that he and all his family can boast about finding your magic cloak. People love boasting – even birds do!"

"You're right," said Hey-Presto, and he turned to the excited little chaffinch. He spoke very solemnly.

"As your reward for finding my pink

cloak you may tell everyone in the world!" he said. "You may shout the news at the top of your voice year after year!"

And, believe it or not, from that day to this every chaffinch shouts out the news each spring and summer. You *must* listen, you really must.

"Pink!" he calls loudly. "PINK, PINK, PINK!"

Listen for him, will you, and call out, "Clever bird! Who found the magic cloak? What colour was it?"

And he will put his knowing little head on one side and answer you at once.

"Pink! PINK-PINK-PINK!"

How John got his ducklings

John and his sister Mary liked playing on their uncle's farm next door. Best of all they liked the baby animals and birds. John was always wanting some for his very, very own. But his Uncle Tom wouldn't let him have any.

"No, John," he said. "You'd forget to feed them or something. Wait till you're old enough."

"But, Uncle, I'm old enough now," said John. "I would feed them and water them well, and Mary would help me. Just let me have two or three yellow chicks for my own, or some of those little yellow ducks. *Do*, Uncle." But Uncle Tom shook his head, and John knew it was no use saying any more.

So he contented himself with trying to help feed the animals, and running after Jim, the yardman, when he went to make the pig-meal or hen food. But he longed to have something that was really and truly his own.

One day Jim went to cart hay for the barn. John and Mary thought they would cart hay too. John had a little wooden cart and wooden horse. He could fill the cart with hay and then pull it along by dragging the horse after him. Mary would help him to put the hay in the barn just like Jim was doing.

So he piled hay into his wooden cart. When John had filled the cart he picked up the string tied to his wooden horse's head and he and Mary pulled it. But dear me, the horse caught its wooden stand against a stone and the front wheel fell off.

"Oh!" said John, in dismay. "It's broken! Poor old Dobbin! I'll take you to Jim. Perhaps he can mend you for me tonight."

He took the horse from the cart and ran off to find Jim, while Mary wheeled the cartful of hay into a hedge nearby.

"Yes, I'll mend it for you sometime," said Jim. "But not tonight, and not while we're haymaking."

He took the horse from John. By that time it was dinner-time, and he and Mary had to run home to wash. John forgot all about the cartful of hay.

It stayed there quite forgotten until one fine morning when a big white duck found the cart under the hedge. Summer flowers had grown over it and it was very hard to see.

When she spied the hay inside, she climbed into the cart very clumsily and sat down. What a fine place to lay an egg! She laid a beautiful big greeny-grey egg there and then sat on it for a while before she went back to the pond.

Each day the duck came to the little wooden cart and stood under the hedge, and laid a nice big egg there. Soon there were twelve, and the duck looked at them proudly.

She made up her mind to sit on them and keep them warm. She just fitted the wooden cart nicely, and she liked the hay inside because it made such a nice soft nest for her eggs.

John waited and waited for Jim to mend his little wooden horse – and after some weeks Jim did mend it. Then John and Mary had to hunt for John's wooden cart! They had forgotten where they had left it. Nobody had seen it, and it was a puzzle where to look for it.

"John!" called his uncle. "You might look out for ducks' eggs while you're hunting for your cart. I think one of the ducks has been laying away each day, and she may have a nest somewhere."

"I'll look hard," said John.

"You can have the eggs for yourself if you find them," said Uncle Tom.

Oooh! If only John and Mary could find them! But they knew how clever ducks were at laying eggs in places they couldn't find or couldn't get at, so they hadn't much hope of finding them.

Suddenly John remembered where he had left his wooden cart. Of course! He had been carting hay like Jim when his horse had broken. Mary must have left his cart under the hedge with the hay.

Sure enough there was his little wooden cart under the hedge, just where Mary had put it all those weeks ago.

John and Mary ran to it – and a big, fat, white duck flew off the cart, leaving behind a nest of beautiful eggs!

John fitted his horse into the shafts and trotted across the farmyard to where Uncle was working.

"Look!" called John. "She's got a whole lot of eggs! Can I have them? I should think they will soon hatch into ducklings!"

"Well, well!" said Uncle Tom, smiling. "Yes, you can have them, John, since you found them."

One day the eggs hatched into yellow ducklings, twelve of them! They follow John everywhere around the farm.

Does he look after them well? Of course he does!

"I shall always love ducklings best," John says, "because they were the first things I had for my *very* own. And I'll never give my little wooden cart away, because it was there I found the eggs!"

Will and Won't

There were once two brothers. One was called William and the other was called Walter. But their mother said they ought to have been named Will and Won't!

Will would always do anything he was asked, and he did it cheerfully and with a smile. Walter wouldn't. He sulked or sighed or grumbled when his mother asked him to run any errand or do any little job.

"Will always says, 'Yes, I will,' but Walter won't do a thing!" said their mother. "Will and Won't, that's what they are — Will and Won't!"

And, dear me, that's what everyone began to call them. "We'll ask Will," said the girls, when they had lost a ball up on the roof. "He'll get it for us. No good asking Won't. He won't do a thing for anyone!"

Now, one day the boys' mother badly wanted an errand run to the lady who did her washing for her. She lived right at the other end of the town.

"Dear me," thought Mummy. "I hardly like to ask Will to go – he's already got wood in for me this morning, and cleaned out the shed, and run to

133

the grocer's. It doesn't seem fair to ask him to do any more – especially as he's settled down to read his book."

So she called Won't. "Won't! Come here a minute, will you?"

"What for?" called back Won't, rudely.

"You come and see!" said his mother, and Won't had to go. "I want you to go to the lady who does the washing for us," said Mummy. "She said she would have your clean shirts ready for me today."

"Mummy, I can't go all that way!" said Won't, sulkily. "I really can't. Get Will to go."

"He's already done a lot of jobs for me," said Won't's mother, sharply. "It's your turn to do something."

"Always having to do jobs and errands!" grumbled Won't, scowling and making his face very ugly. "Can't a boy have any peace?"

"Look here, my boy, when you belong to a family, you don't only take all the good things, you share in the bothersome ones, too, and you help out when you can," said his mother. "If you don't do that you don't deserve to have a mother to look after you, and a father to work for you! Take-All and Do-Nothing, that's what you are! Now, you turn over a new leaf and do things with a smile, as Will does!"

Won't turned away sulkily. He wanted to finish his jigsaw. It seemed very important to him. He sat down just to see if he could finish it quickly. And, of course, he forgot all about what his mother wanted him to do!

"Won't! You haven't been for our clean shirts," said Will suddenly. "Mummy *will* be upset. She badly wanted our clean shirts for tomorrow."

"Bother! I forgot!" said Won't. "Oh, Will, you go – you know the way better than I do. And I feel tired today."

Will knew quite well that Won't would dawdle along and not get back till dinner was half over, and then his mother would worry. So he jumped up himself.

"All right, I'll go," he said. "But I think you're lazy and selfish, Won't."

He went off quickly, knowing that he would not have much time to get there and back before dinner. He ran all the way and collected the clean shirts. Mrs Harris beamed. She liked Will.

"Look, Will," she said, "you go home the other way, down through the market – because there's a circus coming through the town today and that's the way they're taking. You'll see the elephants pulling the caravans, and maybe catch a glimpse of the clowns, too. And you'll hear the lions roaring in their cage."

"Oh yes – I'll go back that way!" said Will. "Thanks for telling me. How did you know?"

"I've been doing the washing for some of the circus-folk," said Mrs Harris. "That's how I know the circus is coming through the market today. Hurry now!"

Will hurried. It would be such fun to see the bright caravans belonging to the circus and to watch the big elephants pulling them along. He hoped there would be one or two clowns turning somersaults in the procession, too.

The circus was coming through the market-place just as Will got there! It was lovely. The elephants plodded slowly along, and three clowns turned somersaults and shouted merrily as the caravans passed by.

In the middle of the market-place one of the clowns climbed to the top of the drinking fountain there.

"Hey, hey, listen!" he cried. "The circus will open tomorrow night! Grandest circus in the world, four elephants, performing dogs, dancing horses, tightrope walkers, everything you want. Catch! Here are some free tickets! Use them tomorrow night! The circus is here! The circus is here!"

The people scrambled for the free tickets – and one fell right on top of Will! He grabbed at it – and there was the ticket, safe in his hand. Hurray! He could go to the circus! He rushed home to tell his mother.

But when Won't heard about it, how long his face was! "*I* haven't got a ticket," he said. "Just like Will's luck!"

His mother turned round sharply.

"Now you stop grumbling, Won't! It's nothing to do with luck! *You* would have got the ticket if you'd done as I told you and done the errand! Your laziness and selfishness stopped you seeing the procession and catching the free ticket. Will deserves it and – mark my words, Won't – unless you change your ways, this is the sort of thing that will happen to you all your life long! If you *won't* do things for others, you *won't* get the fun and excitement and treats that unselfish people get! Will will get everything and deserve it – and Won't won't!"

It served Won't right, didn't it? Will is going to the circus, and Won't will be left behind. But I really don't feel in the least sorry for him, do you?

Mr Stamp-About and the stick

Mr Stamp-About was in one of his tempers. "Who's taken my walking-stick?" he roared. "It's gone! Wait till I find out who's got it!" and he stamped his foot as hard as he could.

"Now, now, Mr Stamp-About, sir," said the milkman, who had just come to the door with his bottle of milk. "Don't take on so! You'll stamp a hole in the floor!"

"And why shouldn't I?" roared Stamp-About. "It's *my* floor, isn't it? Where's that walking-stick of mine? Have *you* seen it?"

"No, and if I had it wouldn't have been a *walking*-stick, I bet it would have been a *running-away* stick, seeing you in such a temper!" grinned the milkman, and dodged as old Stamp-About threw a loaf of bread at him. "Oh, thank you, I'll take that loaf home to my hens!" And away he went, laughing.

What rages old Stamp-About did get into, to be sure!

Now, when Stamp-About went out that morning he felt quite peculiar without his stick. He didn't need it to help him to *walk* – he liked to use it to hit the heads off daisies or dandelions, or to shake at a shouting boy! He certainly missed his stick!

He went over the fields, grumbling to himself. "That rude milkman! And what was it the postman said to me yesterday – that it was a good thing they couldn't put me inside a cannon, or I'd explode and blow it to bits. Where's my stick? What CAN have happened to my stick?"

Now, as he came to the stile, he saw something beside it. It looked like a stick. In fact, it *was* a stick! Stamp-About picked it up at once.

"Ha! A walking-stick! All by itself. And a good strong one, too. What's this on the top of the handle – a carving of some sort? A head – the head of a cheeky-looking fellow, too. Beautifully carved! I wonder who the stick belongs to?"

He tucked it under his arm and went off with it. If he heard that anyone had lost it he'd give it to them.

"But someone's taken mine, and I've got to have one for myself," thought Stamp-About. "And whoever owns this shouldn't have been careless enough to leave it about. Serve him right if he comes back and can't find it!"

He went home with the stick, feeling pleased with it. It was just the right size for him, very strong, and certainly that little head was most beautifully carved.

"Though I don't like the way it looks at me," thought Stamp-About. "Too cheeky for anything!" He stood it in

the corner of his room, and went to get himself a meal. Ah, there was plenty of that meat pie left. Good!

Just as he was putting it on the table, he heard a knock at the door, and a voice said, "Stamp-About, are you in? I've come to dinner with you!"

"That's old Cousin Gubbins!" thought Stamp-About crossly. "He'll eat half the pie! Well, I shan't open the door. Let him think I'm out."

He hid behind the cupboard door, in case Gubbins looked in at the window and saw him. Gubbins banged at the door again. And then Stamp-About was amazed to hear a thin, high voice calling out clearly, "Come in! He's at home!"

And Cousin Gubbins at once opened the door and came in. He looked round to see where the voice had come from, and saw Stamp-About behind the cupboard door.

"Hello, what are you doing there?" said Gubbins in astonishment.

"Hiding! *He, he!*" said the same little

high voice, and laughed and laughed.

Stamp-About was very angry. Now his cousin Gubbins had come in, after all ... and there was somebody in his kitchen being very, very annoying. Where did that voice come from? He simply couldn't imagine.

"I've come to dinner, Stamp-About," said Gubbins. "You've had three meals with me in three weeks – now it's my turn to have a meal with you."

"I've nothing to offer you," said Stamp-About, in a surly voice.

"Ooooooh! You've forgotten that meat pie!" said the little high voice. "Ooooh – you fibber!"

Stamp-About stared round the room. *WHO* had said that? There was nobody there except Stamp-About himself and his greedy cousin. He felt very uncomfortable. Was the voice real? Yes it must be, because Gubbins had heard it too.

"Ha – meat pie! Just what I feel like!" said Gubbins and sat down.

Stamp-About had to put the pie on the table, and the two made a good meal of it.

"There's a pudding in the larder," remarked the little high voice, after a bit. "*He, he* – you do look cross, Stamp-About!"

"Who's saying all these silly things?" roared Stamp-About, losing his temper.

"Do you suppose it's that stick over in the corner?" asked Gubbins, grinning. "The little head at the top has been winking at me ever since I sat down at the table."

"What!" cried Stamp-About, and stared over at the stick.

Yes – the little head was winking at him, too, and its small carved mouth smiled.

"Stamp-About stole me," said the stick.

"Oooh, what a story! I didn't!" said Stamp-About, angrily.

"Yes, you did. You should have taken me to the police station, but you didn't," said the little high voice. "I belong to Mr Spell-Maker. My word – whatever will he do to you when he knows you stole me from that stile? He was coming back for me, I know he was. He just left me there by mistake."

Stamp-About stared at the stick in horror. So it belonged to Mr Spell-Maker – and Mr Spell-Maker had just as bad a temper as Stamp-About.

"I'll take you to the police station at once," he said, and went over to the stick.

But it jumped into the air. "No!" it said. "I don't want to go there. I'll wait till my master finds out I'm here, and watch what he does to you. *He, he* – I once saw him turn a witch into an ice-cream."

Stamp-About was really scared. He snatched up the stick at once, and tucked it firmly under his arm. "You'd better come with me, Cousin Gubbins," he said.

"No, no," said Gubbins. "I'll just stay

and finish my meal. I'll look in the larder for the pudding."

Stamp-About groaned and went off to the police station. Before he got there the little carved wooden head under his arm had nipped him!

"Let me go!" it cried. "I'll nip you again!"

Stamp-About wasn't going to have that. He took out his handkerchief and tied it round the stick's carved head. "There!" he said. "Now you can't say a word!"

He took the stick to the police station. "I found it in a field," he said. "You'd better ask Mr Spell-Maker if it belongs to him. I don't want it. It's a rude stick, and spiteful, too!"

And away he went home, leaving the surprised policeman undoing the handkerchief from the stick's carved head. How amazed he was when the stick hit him on the shins and then tried to hop away. The policeman promptly locked it in a cell.

Stamp-About was most relieved to have left the stick behind. He hurried home, hoping to get there before Gubbins had eaten everything in the larder. But Gubbins had gone – and so had all the food except for half a loaf of stale bread!

Stamp-About went out to buy a cake for his tea. When he got back, he sat down for a snooze, and began to snore a little. He woke up very suddenly, to hear a little high voice say "Don't snore like that! I don't like it!"

And there was the stick again, standing by the fireplace, its little head glaring crossly at him.

"How did you get back here?" said Stamp-About, horrified.

"I didn't like the police station, so I just wriggled out between the bars of my cell," said the stick. "It was easy. Let me lean against your knee in front of the fire. I'll be nice and warm then."

"*No*," said Stamp-About, and got a rap on his leg that made him jump.

That stick could certainly be mean!

"I shall hit your knee-cap next if you try to move me," said the little carved head.

"You're a most extraordinary stick," Stamp-About said in amazement. "Did Mr Spell-Maker carve you?"

"Yes, then he rubbed a spell on my head so that I could talk," said the stick. "I wonder what he'll do to you when he knows *you've* got me!"

Stamp-About felt most alarmed again. He got up at once. "I'll throw you away in the river, and let you float for miles to the sea!" he said angrily.

The stick hopped away at once, over the kitchen floor, but Stamp-About chased it till he caught it. He tied a string to it and then, dragging it behind him so that it couldn't hit him, he set off to the river. *Splash*! He threw the stick into it, and sighed in relief. Why had he brought such a nasty, mean thing home with him? Well, that was the end of it.

He went back home and sat down to

finish his snooze in his arm chair – but would you believe it, he hadn't been asleep for more than half an hour when he felt something hit his knee. And then he felt something slithering all the way up him and down again. He opened his eyes in a hurry.

It was the carved stick back again! It was dripping wet and was wiping itself dry on Stamp-About's clothes.

"I jumped out of the river! I jumped out!" it said, in its little high voice. "It was cold and wet. Let me get into your warm pocket! Let me get behind your cosy waistcoat. What, you won't let me! Then I'll hit you!"

Stamp-About was really in despair. He stared at the wriggling stick in horror. Should he bury it? No, it might take root and grow into even more mean sticks. Should he put it into his dustbin? No, it would probably rattle the lid till someone let it out.

Well, then – there was only one thing left to do! He would take it back to

Mr Spell-Maker. He would be delighted to have it back, and Stamp-About would then have got rid of the annoying stick once and for all! He put the stick on the cushion in his chair and went to the cupboard. He found a nice long box, that had once had an umbrella in. He put some cotton wool in it and called to the stick.

"Here you are! I've made a nice, cosy, comfy bed for you, Stick! Cuddle down in this cotton wool, and you will soon be dry and warm!"

"Ah, now you're being sensible!" said the little wooden head, grinning, and the stick hopped over to the box. "Yes, it looks good. I'll lie down and get dry and warm."

The stick jumped into the long, narrow box and tucked itself into the wool. In a trice Stamp-About clapped the lid on and tied string tightly round it.

"Aha!" he said. "Got you! Now I'm taking you back to Mr Spell-Maker.

I've no doubt you will be very glad to hear that. You're not going to have any chance of rapping my shins though. You can stay quite still in this box!"

But that's just what the carved stick wouldn't do! It jiggled about, rapped against the lid, and cried out loudly in its high little voice. As Stamp-About carried the box down the road, everyone stared in amazement.

"Whatever *have* you got in that box?" said old Dame Hurry-By. "If it's some poor animal, you let it out at once!"

Stamp-About didn't stop until he came to Mr Spell-Maker's little pointed house on the top of the hill. He rapped on the door. "Mr Spell-Maker! I've brought back your stick!"

Old Mr Spell-Maker put his head out of the window. "For goodness sake! I left it by the stile because I never wanted to see it again. It's a perfect nuisance of a stick. *I* don't want it!"

He slammed the window. Stamp-

About heard the stick laughing and, in a rage, he opened the front door and flung the box inside. Then he slammed the door and went off down the hill at top speed. He was *not* going to have that stick again.

But soon he heard a little high voice shouting breathlessly to him. "Wait! Wait! Mr Spell-Maker says you can have me. I slid out of the letter-box. Wait! Wait!"

But Stamp-About didn't wait. He rushed home and went to shut himself in his garden-shed.

No sooner was he in the shed than he saw his own dear old stick, carved with a dog's head on top, the one he had lost! Well, well, well, of course, he had left it in the shed the day before. He picked it up in delight and just at that very moment the other stick came rapping at the shed door.

Stamp-About opened it, his own stick in his hand. In came the other stick, complaining bitterly. "Why did you

leave me? I've come to live with *you* now. Oh, what's that?"

"My *own* stick!" roared Stamp-About. "See the dog's head on top? Do you want it to chase you and bite you? *Grrrrrrr!*"

Stamp-About growled so exactly like a dog that the first stick hopped away hurriedly down the garden path.

"No, no!" it cried. "No, no!"

And that was the last time that Stamp-About ever heard the carved head's little high voice.

Goodness knows where the stick went to. Stamp-About is so afraid it may come back that he's paying Mr Spell-Maker to put special magic on his own stick, to make it bark. That will scare away any other stick – and burglars, too. I wouldn't mind a stick like that myself! It would really be very useful!

Mister Quink's garden

Once upon a time, not very long ago, Mr Brown took his family for a day in the country. There were Mrs Brown, the mother, Annie Brown, the little girl, and Tommy Brown, the little boy.

"We'll all go, every one of us," said Mr Brown. "The country is lovely now. We shall enjoy it. Take enough food for the whole day, Mummy."

So Mrs Brown cut ham sandwiches and tomato sandwiches, and packed them into cardboard boxes. She took two bottles of lemon barley water. She packed four oranges and four bananas into a basket with the bottles. She took a large tin of fruit salad, and four cardboard plates and spoons to

eat it with. And last of all she took
four bars of chocolate and a bag of
peppermints.

So you can see that the Brown family
meant to have a good feast. It was a
lovely day when they set off in the
bus. The sun shone brightly. The sky
was as blue as the bluebells that were
beginning to peep in the woods. The
birds in the hedges sang merrily and
the banks were yellow with primroses.

Mrs Brown was happy. She sat in
the bus and looked at everything.
Mr Brown was happy too. The children
looked out for an ice-cream man with
his van, for they each had some money
to spend and they wanted ice-cream.
They were happy too.

They got off the bus at last and
walked into the woods. The sun was
so hot that they were glad of the shade.
Tommy and Annie danced on in front,
shouting to their mother to look at the
bluebells. Mr and Mrs Brown carried
the bags and basket.

"Look for a nice place to sit, Annie," called Mrs Brown.

Presently they found one. It was the prettiest place in the wood – and, although they did not know it, it was really the garden belonging to Mister Quink, the old brownie. He lived in the old oak tree under whose branches the Brown family sat. He had a close-fitting door in the trunk of the tree and a small window with a tiny curtain of moss. Nobody ever knew he lived there – except the little folk of course – because Mister Quink never showed himself to ordinary people.

Now Mister Quink was very proud of his garden and he worked there every night. There was a tiny stream running through it, and he had planted flowers neatly along each side. He had arranged cushions of moss here and there in his garden too, so that his friends might sit on them when they came to visit him. He had three patches of bluebells, the finest in the wood – and one special secret plant which always grew a *white* bluebell, which, as you know, is a very lucky flower.

Mister Quink had made a little bower of honeysuckle leaves in one corner, and a nook of violets grew close by, so that whoever sat in the nook could smell the sweet scent of the hidden violets. Everything in the garden was neat and tidy and beautiful.

No wonder the Browns thought it was lovely! Mr and Mrs Brown sat down under the tree and put their basket and bags by them. They didn't know they were in a brownie's garden, because Mister Quink had no fence or wall or hedge round it. The children wanted to have something to eat at once.

"Well, we'll have our dinner now," said Mrs Brown, and she began to unpack the things. Soon they were all munching happily. They drank the lemon barley water. It was delicious.

"Let's put the bottles up over there and throw stones at them," said

Mr Brown. "We'll break them."

"But won't the broken pieces be dangerous?" said Mrs Brown.

"Pooh! Who will ever come here?" said Mr Brown.

So they set up the bottles and threw stones at them, and soon the two bottles were smashed to bits, and pieces of glass lay all over the little dell. Mr Brown unfolded his newspaper. "Now I'm going to have a rest," he said. "Don't disturb me, children."

Little by little the lovely garden belonging to Mister Quink began to look dreadful. The brownie peeped out of his tiny window in the oak tree and saw with dismay all that was happening.

He saw Mrs Brown peel oranges for the children and throw the peel on the grass. He saw the children eating bananas and throwing the skins at one another – for they were not very well-behaved children. He saw Mr Brown throw his banana skin into the honeysuckle bower.

The Brown family stayed there all the afternoon. It was so peaceful, and the birds sang so sweetly. They had their tea there too – and soon it was time to go home.

Mrs Brown looked round at the mess, and couldn't help feeling a bit sorry about it.

"Are there any litter bins or baskets anywhere?" she asked. "Perhaps we ought to put this mess into one."

"There aren't any, Mummy," said Tommy. "This is quite a wild part of the wood. I don't suppose anyone comes here but us. All the same, our teacher always tells us at school not to spoil the country – do you suppose we ought to take our rubbish back home with us?"

"I'm not carrying back all that litter," said Mr Brown at once. He was rather a selfish man. "Leave it here. No one will ever know."

"Mummy, let's take these bluebells home with us," cried Annie. "And let's dig up these primroses and violets by the root, and some of this moss. They'll look lovely in our garden at home!"

So they dug up Mister Quink's finest primroses and violets and moss, and picked all his bluebells – and then they found the lucky white bluebell! So they dug up its bulb and put that in the basket too. Then home they went.

Mister Quink opened his front door and crept out. When he saw his beautiful garden scattered with broken glass, orange peel, banana skins, cardboard boxes, empty bags, chocolate paper and sheets of newspaper – when he saw his lovely plants gone and his moss spoilt, he sat down on a stone and cried big tears.

But when he found his white bluebell gone he was very angry! He called a meeting of all the brownies in the wood and they came to see his spoilt garden.

Most of them had complaints and grumbles too.

"Some people left all their horrid paper bags in my field the other day," said Nod, an old brownie.

"And some boys threw broken bottles into my stream, and I scratched my foot when I paddled there," said Doolin, a small, bright-eyed brownie.

"But these Browns are the worst of the lot," said Mister Quink fiercely. "Look at this mess! Whatever shall I do with it?"

"The Browns have a neat little garden," said Hoodle, a sharp-eyed brownie who travelled a good deal. "As all this mess belongs to them, why not take it back to them and put it into their own garden?"

"That's a good idea!" said all the brownies at once. "They don't seem to mind litter and rubbish and mess — so maybe they won't bother about broken bottles and papers and peel in their own garden."

"I can give them about six old newspapers I've picked up from my field at one time and another," said Nod.

"And I can give them a sackful of broken glass," said Doolin.

"We'll go tonight and dump everything in the Browns' garden," said everyone. "Just the thing! How pleased they will be to get such a nice lot of rubbish back!"

So that night seven brownies all made their way from the wood and rode on the back of the midnight owl who flies to and from the town. When they got to the Browns' garden they landed on the grass and opened their sacks.

They shook out the glass all over the neat lawn. They threw the newspapers where the wind could blow them around. They scattered the paper and boxes and peel and skin here and there. And just as they were going, Mister Quink stopped short and pointed to something.

"Look!" he said. "My lucky white bluebell! I must take that back with me."

"And see – here's a lupin plant just flowering!" said Nod. "I haven't one of those at home. As the Browns took your flowers, Quink, they probably wouldn't mind us taking theirs. I *must* have that lupin!"

In a few minutes the brownies were digging up all the finest things in the Browns' garden, and then off they went again on the owl, their sacks empty of rubbish but full now of lovely plants. The brownies were delighted.

In the morning, when Mr Brown awoke and looked out of the window to see what sort of a day it was, he got *such* a shock! His garden was a perfect wreck! His favourite plants were gone – his lawn was scattered with broken glass – and all kinds of rubbish blew about or lay on the beds.

"Just look at that!" said Mr Brown fiercely. "Just look at that. Now who's done that, I should like to know!"

Mrs Brown jumped out of bed and gazed at the dreadful garden. Tears came into her eyes, for she loved her little garden. "Oh, how could anyone be so horrid!" she said.

Tommy and Annie were angry too. "What a terrible mess," said Annie. "Why don't people clear up their litter properly instead of throwing it into *our* garden?"

Well, Mr Brown told the policeman, and the policeman wrote a lot of things down in his notebook and said he would keep a watch on the garden and see it didn't happen again. And Tommy and Annie spent the whole morning clearing up the mess and making the garden neat. Mr Brown had to buy more plants in place of the ones that had gone, and he was very angry about it.

Well, will you believe it, although the policeman watched carefully the next night, *some*body he didn't see came and emptied all sorts of rubbish in the Browns' garden again! It was most extraordinary because although the policeman saw the rubbish being thrown about the garden he couldn't see who was throwing it!

The brownies were invisible to him, for he didn't believe in fairies. He was frightened and ran all the way back to the police station.

And do you know, the brownies still come every other night or so and give to the Browns all the rubbish that people leave about the countryside. Their garden is a dreadful sight and they can't do anything about it.

Annie is beginning to wonder if it *can* be the little folk who are doing it – and she wishes the Browns hadn't been so untidy in the wood that day!

"I shall put up a notice to say we're sorry and won't spoil the country again," said Annie to herself. "Then the little folk will stop bringing us rubbish."

So she is going to do that tonight – and then the brownies will have to choose someone else's garden. I hope it won't be yours! But I'm sure you are not like the Browns, are you? You know how to behave when you go to the country, so *your* garden will be safe!

Brer Rabbit has some fun!

Old Brer Terrapin came down Brer
Rabbit's front path as fast as he
could waddle, and that was very slow
indeed.

He called as he came. "Hello, Brer
Rabbit, you gone to market yet? You
at home?"

Brer Rabbit opened the door. He had
his basket on his arm, all ready to go
and do his marketing.

"What's turned you into a racehorse,
old Brer Terrapin?" he said. "I've never
seen you rattle along like this before."

"Listen, Brer Rabbit," said Brer
Terrapin, "I was under a bush near Brer
Bear's just now, and I heard him tell old
Mrs Bear that he was going to lie in

wait for you when you came back from market, and take your goods. He says you cheeked him yesterday, and he's going to show you what happens when people call him names."

"I only said he was an old snuffle-snout and a puffle-plonk," said Brer Rabbit.

"Whatever are they?" asked Brer Terrapin with interest. "You do think up some odd names, Brer Rabbit."

"I don't know *what* they are," said Brer Rabbit. "I just thought they suited Brer Bear when he's snuffing and puffing around. Oho – so he thinks he's going to steal my goods, does he,

when I come back from market?"

"Yes. And I've almost cracked my shell coming along here to tell you," said Brer Terrapin. "I shan't be able to walk another step today."

"You're a friend," said Brer Rabbit, "a real friend, but you'll have to do another bit of walking today all the same, Brer Terrapin. I'm going to pay old Brer Bear back for his mean little plan – and you've got to help."

"What do you want me to do?" asked Brer Terrapin, who felt that all *he* wanted to do was to sit down and put his head under his shell and go to sleep.

"Nothing much. Just be along by the old hollow tree not far from Brer Bear's house at half-past three this afternoon," said Brer Rabbit. "And carry an empty basket on your back for me. Will you do that? And I'll want you to have supper with me tonight, because there'll be chicken, and carrot soup and lettuce pie."

"Sounds good!" said Brer Terrapin.

"Right, Brer Rabbit, I'll be along by the old hollow tree. But you be careful of Brer Bear. He's in a temper, he is, and you know what kind of claws he's got!"

"Brer Bear will have to look after himself if he tries to get the better of *me*," said Brer Rabbit, "claws or no claws. Well, I'm off to market now, Brer Terrapin. See you later!"

He went off with his shopping basket, whistling like a blackbird. He shopped at the market, and bought a whole lot of things he wanted. Yes, Brer Rabbit was a good spender when he had the money!

At three o'clock he was on his way home, with a full basket, and a bag that also looked full of something. When he came to the hollow tree he gave a low whistle. Out came old Brer Terrapin, an empty basket balanced on his shell.

Brer Rabbit took the empty basket and put his full one on Brer Terrapin's back. "Can you carry that?" he said. "It's got our supper for tonight in it, and a few other things as well."

"My shell could carry a cartload," boasted Brer Terrapin. "It's as strong as iron. What am I to do now? Carry this basket home for you?"

"That's right," said Brer Rabbit. "And I'm going to walk right in front of Brer Bear's house so that he can see me and come after me."

"He's not there," said Brer Terrapin. "He's hiding in the bushes near the river."

"Better and better!" said Brer Rabbit.

He began to take some things out of the bag he carried and put them into the empty basket. They were all done up in neat little parcels.

"What are those for?" asked Brer Terrapin.

"Oh, nice little presents for Brer Bear!" said Brer Rabbit. "A packet of old nails – a piece of iron – two nice heavy stones – a big old bone – and the broken head of an axe. I picked them up from the rubbish at the market."

Brer Terrapin chuckled. "I'd rather

have you for my friend than my enemy, Brer Rabbit," he said, "and that's the truth. Well, I'll be off. It'll take me a long time to get to your house, carrying this basket."

He went off through the wood, and Brer Rabbit, carrying the other basket full of wrapped-up rubbish, went whistling by Brer Bear's house. He went towards the river, where the bridge was, keeping a sharp look-out for old Brer Bear. Ah – he must be in that bush. He was hidden except for one large foot he had forgotten about. It was sticking out of the bottom of the bush.

Just as he came up to the bush Brer Bear leapt out at him. Brer Rabbit gave a yell and dodged. He ran towards the river, and Brer Bear lumbered after him at top speed.

Brer Rabbit pretended to catch his foot on a tree-root, and almost fell. When he went on again he was limping, and groaning loudly. Brer Bear was most delighted.

Brer Rabbit turned and called out to Brer Bear. "Don't you chase me now, Brer Bear. You can see I'm limping. What are you chasing me for?"

"That basket of goods!" shouted Brer Bear. "And limp or no limp, I'm going to catch you and get that basket."

Brer Rabbit limped along, still groaning and with a wicked twinkle in his eye. He was almost at the river now, and Brer Bear was just behind him, puffing like a steam-engine.

Brer Rabbit turned and faced him. "You *shan't* have my goods!" he shouted, and threw his basket straight into the river nearby. *Splash!* The basket hit the water and disappeared.

Brer Bear gave a yell of dismay. He went to the bank and peered down into the river. He could quite clearly see the basket resting on the bed of the stream.

"You think you've got the best of me, Brer Rabbit, don't you?" said Brer Bear, taking off his coat. "Well, you haven't. I'm going to wade into the water and

get that basket out before everything's soaked. I'll dry the goods and keep them! That will teach you to call me names!"

"I don't need anyone to teach me to call you names," said Brer Rabbit. "I can think of plenty more myself. *You* won't be able to get that basket, old Puff-and-Blow!"

Brer Bear snorted. He took off his shoes and put his walking stick down by his coat. Then he waded into the water.

"Is it cold, Snuffly-Snout?" asked Brer Rabbit, standing on the bridge to watch.

Brer Bear snorted again. He was getting in quite deep now, and the water certainly *was* very cold.

"A bit more to the right, Puffle-Plonk," said Brer Rabbit helpfully. "Mind that hole – oooch – you're in it! Hold up, Puff-and-Blow, hold up!"

Brer Bear didn't feel the cold anymore, because he was now boiling with anger. That Brer Rabbit! That – that – oh dear, what a pity he wasn't as good as Brer Rabbit at thinking up names. He came at last to the basket, bent down too far, got the water up his nose, and spluttered.

"Now then, Splutter-Gulp!" said Brer Rabbit. "Do be careful!"

Brer Bear had got the basket at last. My, how heavy it was! Brer Rabbit had certainly been shopping that morning.

Aha – his own larder would be full in a very short while!

He took the basket to the bank. He shook himself vigorously to get the water off his thick fur. Then he sat down and began to open the parcels in the basket.

Stones! And old bones! Nails! A bit of iron! An old axe-head! Why – why – what was all this? *This* wasn't shopping goods, *this* wasn't . . .

Brer Bear got to his feet, suddenly feeling very angry. It was a trick! A mean trick! A trick to get him into the river and make him as wet as could be. Now where was that rascal of a rabbit? He would just get hold of him and shake him till his ears fell off!

But Brer Rabbit was away in the distance *hoppity-skip* – and what was more, he was wearing Brer Bear's coat, he had Brer Bear's shoes round his neck, and he was twirling Brer Bear's new walking stick as he went! Now to find Brer Terrapin!

Brer Terrapin was very pleased to see Brer Rabbit. He had just arrived at the house when Brer Rabbit himself came skipping along like a week-old lamb, twirling Brer Bear's walking stick.

"Brer Bear's soaked through," he told Brer Terrapin. "Wading in the river on a cold day like this – dear, dear, how foolish people are. Going after a lot of rubbish, too! Well, Brer Terrapin, I feel like a dinner party tonight – we'll send out a few invitations."

So they did, and everyone was most delighted to come. Even Brer Bear was asked but, of course, he didn't come. Not he! He had had enough of Brer Rabbit for one day.

"Brer Bear is the only one who hasn't turned up," said Brer Rabbit, beaming round at his guests. "I'm so sorry."

"He's in bed with a bad cold," said Brer Possum. "A very *very* bad cold, poor fellow."

"Dear me!" said Brer Rabbit. "Now – I *do* wonder how he got that?"

Brer Rabbit is so cunning!

Once, when Brer Rabbit was trotting along over a field, the wind blew some dead leaves out of the ditch into his face. Brer Rabbit got a real fright, and he tore off as if a hundred dogs were after him!

Well, it happened that Brer Fox and Brer Bear saw him running away, and they laughed to think that a few leaves had frightened Brer Rabbit. They went about among all the animals, telling them what a coward Brer Rabbit was, and how he had run away because of a few leaves.

When people met Brer Rabbit after that, they grinned slyly, and asked him whether he had had any more frights.

Brer Rabbit got very tired of it. "I'm as brave as any of you!" he said. "Yes, and braver too!"

"Well, show us what a brave man you are, then!" cried everyone, and they giggled at Brer Rabbit's angry face.

Brer Rabbit went off in a temper, and he thought and thought how he might show everyone that he was a brave fellow. Then he grinned and slapped his knee.

"I'll soon show them!" he chuckled. "My, they'll get a fright, but it will serve them right!"

Then Brer Rabbit went to work out his idea. He took seven of his tin plates, made a hole in the middle of each, and threaded them together on a thick string. My, what a noise they made when he shook the string!

Then he took a big piece of glass from his cucumber-frame and ran his wet paw up and down it to see if it would make a good noise. It did! Oh, what a squeaking, squealing noise it made!

Brer Rabbit grinned to himself.

Well, that night Brer Rabbit took the string of tin plates and the piece of glass with him and climbed up a tree not far

183

from Brer Fox's house. When he was comfortably settled, he began to enjoy himself.

He moaned and howled like twenty cats. He yelped like a dozen dogs. He screeched like a hundred parrots. "*Oh-ee-oo-ee, ie-oh-ee-oh, YOW, YOW, YOW!*"

Then he shook the string hard that joined the tin plates together, and they all jangled through the quiet night as if a thousand dustbins had gone mad and were dancing in a ring. *Clang, jang, clang, jang, clinky, clanky, clang, JANG!*

Brer Rabbit nearly fell out of the tree laughing at the awful noise he made. Next, he took the big piece of glass, wet his paw, and began to run it up and down the glass. *EEEEEEEE-OOOO, EEEEEEEE-OOOOO!* it went, and all the wakened animals round him shivered and shook to hear such a dreadful squealing noise.

Then Brer Rabbit jangled his plates

again. *Clang, jang, clang, jang, clinky, clanky, clang, jang!*

Brer Fox was sitting up in bed, as scared as could be. He couldn't for the life of him imagine what the noise was. It was like nothing he had ever heard before.

Brer Wolf was hiding under his bed. Brer Bear and Mrs Bear were clinging together, crying on each other's shoulders they were so frightened.

All the other animals were trembling, too, wondering what was going to happen next.

"*YOW, YOW, YOW!*" yelled Brer Rabbit. *Clinkity, clang, jang!* went his tin plates. *EeeeeeEEeeeeEEE-ooooo!* went his paw, squeaking up the glass.

At last Brer Rabbit hopped down from his tree, ran to a tumbledown shed nearby, put all his things there, and then made his way to Brer Fox's house. He knocked loudly on the door, *BLIM, BLAM!*

Brer Fox got such a shock that he fell

out of bed. "Who's there?" he said in a trembling voice.

"Me, Brer Rabbit," said Brer Rabbit. "I've come to see what all the noise is about."

"Oh Brer Rabbit, dear Brer Rabbit, I'm so glad to see you," said Brer Fox, almost falling over himself to open the door. "Do come in. I've been scared out of my life. Whatever is that noise, do you think?"

"I don't know," said Brer Rabbit untruthfully. "Unless it is old Brer Elephant rampaging around, making a frightful noise. I just came to see if you were all right, Brer Fox."

"Well, that's mighty kind of you, Brer Rabbit," said Brer Fox. "I wonder you're not afraid to be out, with all that noise around. What are you going to do now? Don't leave me!"

"I'm just off to see if Brer Wolf and Brer Bear are all right," said Brer Rabbit. "Maybe they are scared and will be glad to see me."

Off he went, and found Brer Wolf and Brer Bear just as scared as Brer Fox. My, they thought he was a very brave fellow to be out that night!

"We'll look in the morning and see if we can see any signs of Brer Elephant," said Brer Rabbit. "It's a wet and muddy night and maybe we'll find his footprints. Then we can follow them and see where he is!"

After Brer Rabbit had left his friends, he skipped and danced a bit with glee, and then he went to where he had hidden a big round log of wood, just the shape of an elephant's great foot. Brer Rabbit went all round about Brer Fox's house and Brer Bear's and Brer Wolf's, stamping the end of the big log into the mud, so that it looked for all the world as if a mighty big lot of feet had been going around there in the night.

Brer Rabbit giggled to himself when he had finished. He went back home to bed and slept well till morning.

The next day he and all the other

animals went to look for footprints. When the others saw the enormous marks in the mud they were as scared as could be.

"Those are an elephant's marks all right!" said Brer Fox. "I know an elephant's marks when I see them. My, he was around here last night all right. I wonder he didn't knock my house down!"

"Let's follow the footprints and see where they go to," said Brer Rabbit.

"I don't think I want to do that," said Brer Bear, who didn't like the look of things at all.

"What! Are you afraid?" cried Brer Rabbit. "Well, *I'm* not! I'm going to see where these footmarks lead to even if I have to go alone!"

Well, he followed the footprints in the mud, and they led him to the old tumbledown shed, as he knew they would, for he had put them there himself! Brer Fox and the others followed him at a good distance. Brer

Rabbit tiptoed to the shed and looked inside.

"Yes," said the cunning fellow, "he's in there all right! Fast asleep! I think I'll go and attack him while he's asleep!"

"What! Attack an elephant!" said Brer Wolf in the greatest astonishment. "Don't be silly."

"*I'm* not afraid of elephants!" said Brer Rabbit. "I'll go in and bang him on the head! I guess he'll rush out in a mighty hurry, so be careful he doesn't knock you all over!"

"Come back, Brer Rabbit!" called Brer Fox, as Brer Rabbit tiptoed to the shed again. "You'll only make him angry and he'll rush out and knock down all our houses!"

Brer Rabbit disappeared into the shed. He had a good laugh and then he began. He took up his string of tin plates and made them dance with a *clanky-lanky clang-jang!* He made his paw squeal up and down the glass. He yowled and howled. He took a tin trumpet from his pocket and blew hard, for he had once heard that elephants made a trumpeting sound.

Then he began to shout and yell in his own voice, "Take *that*, you great noisy creature! Take *that*, you stupid elephant! And that, and that, and that!"

Every time he said, "And *that*!" Brer Rabbit hit the side of the shed with a piece of wood and it made a terrible noise. *Crash! Crash! Crash!*

The animals waiting not far off shivered and shook. Brer Rabbit put his eye to a crack in the wall of the shed and grinned to see them.

Then he took a heap of paper bags out of his pocket, and blew them up one by one. He banged them with his hand and they went *POP!*

POP! POP! POP! POP! They sounded like guns shooting. Brer Rabbit jangled his plates again, and banged the shed with the piece of wood. You might have thought that at least twenty animals were fighting inside that shed!

And then Brer Rabbit took up the log that he had made the footprints with and sent it crashing through the other side of the shed, as if some big animal had fallen through it and was scrambling away. He began to shout.

"Run, Brer Elephant, run!" he yelled. "Run, or I'll get you! Run, run!"

Brer Fox, Brer Wolf, and all the others thought that the elephant had crashed its way out of the shed and was loose. At once they fled to Brer Fox's house and bolted themselves in, trembling. Brer Rabbit saw them from the crack in the shed and laughed fit to kill himself.

When at last he stopped laughing he made his way to Brer Fox's house, panting as if he had been having a great fight. He knocked at the door, *Blam, blam!*

"Who's there?" called Brer Fox, afraid.

"Brer Rabbit," said Brer Rabbit in a big voice. The door opened and all the

191

animals came out. They crowded round Brer Rabbit, patted him on the back, hugged him and fussed him! My, it was grand for Brer Rabbit!

"You're a hero!" cried Brer Fox.

"The bravest creature in the world!" said Brer Bear.

"The strongest of us all!" said Brer Wolf.

"I'm glad you think so, friends," said Brer Rabbit. "There was a time when you called me a coward, and maybe if I remember which of you laughed at me then, I might treat them as I treated old Brer Elephant!"

"*We* wouldn't laugh at a brave man like Brer Rabbit!" shouted everyone at once.

"Well, just see you don't!" said Brer Rabbit, and he put his nose in the air, threw out his chest, and walked off, looking mighty biggitty! And after that the animals were very careful to be polite to Brer Rabbit for a long, long time!

Mrs Doodle loses her head

Mrs Doodle was a funny sort of person. If anything happened to upset her in any way, she made such a fuss.

When her clothes-line blew down and her washing fell into the mud, how she flapped and fussed!

"Oh, look at that! Oh my, oh my, whatever am I to do? My beautiful washing! What shall I do-oo-ooo?"

"Now don't lose your head," said Mrs Twinks, her next-door neighbour. "Really, I never knew anyone like you, Mrs Doodle, for getting into a flap about nothing!"

"Nothing!" said Mrs Doodle, indignantly, getting redder and redder in the face. "What do you mean – *nothing*? Do you call my clean washing in the mud nothing? Do you call my broken clothes-line nothing? I'd like to know what you would call something!"

It was always like that with Mrs Doodle. She made such a fuss, and got into such a state about things that it was very difficult to calm her down. Her neighbours really got very tired of it.

"She loses her head about everything," said Mrs Twinks to Mrs Gobo. "She really does."

"One day she'll lose it altogether," said Mrs Gobo, with a laugh.

One morning Mrs Doodle put a lot of paper on the fire to burn. It flared up at once, and sent big flames all the way up the chimney. Mrs Doodle hadn't had her chimney swept when she should, and it was full of soot.

The soot caught fire – and at once the flames and smoke swept right up the chimney to the very top! Smoke poured out, black and thick.

Mrs Gobo came banging at Mrs Doodle's door. "Hey! Your chimney is on fire! Hey!"

Mrs Doodle began to pant with worry. She rushed here and she rushed there. She fell over the cat. She cried and wept. But she didn't put out the fire.

"Now don't lose your head," said Mrs Gobo. "Just put some water on the fire and put out the flames. You ought to have had that chimney swept ages ago."

"Oh dear, oh my, oh my, oh dear!" groaned Mrs Doodle, and threw a whole bucketful of water towards the flames in the grate. Unluckily, she didn't throw far enough and soaked the poor cat from head to foot. It jumped in fright and scratched Mrs Doodle by accident as it ran past. She screamed, and ran round and round the kitchen, shouting out to Mrs Gobo!

"Help me, help me! The cat has scratched me, my chimney's on fire, and I don't know what to do."

"Well, you're losing your head as usual," said Mrs Gobo. She put out the fire and then dried the poor frightened cat.

"I don't lose my head," said Mrs Doodle, crossly. "Don't say that. It's a stupid thing to say. I never lose my head about things. I am very sensible."

Mrs Gobo laughed. "Well, well! If that is what you call being sensible, I don't know how you behave when you're silly!"

Mrs Gobo went out. On the way home she met Dame Tip-Tap, who knew a lot of magic. Mrs Gobo told Dame Tip-Tap all about Mrs Doodle.

"She's such a fusser," she said. "I wish we could cure her. She is always losing her head about things."

"Well," said Dame Tip-Tap, with a twinkle in her eye, "I know some magic that makes people's heads disappear. Shall we try it on Mrs Doodle? You understand – her head doesn't *really* go – it's just that we can't see it. It's still there, but can't be seen. Perhaps if I use my magic and make her lose her head like that, it will teach her not to make such a fuss about things."

"Oooh – that would be funny," said Mrs Gobo, with a chuckle. So, the very next time that Mrs Doodle began to squeal and cry and make a fuss, Mrs Gobo hurried along to her house with Dame Tip-Tap.

Dame Tip-Tap flicked a little yellow powder over Mrs Doodle's head when she wasn't looking and muttered some very magic words under her breath. Mrs Doodle was in a great state because her cat had stolen some sausages, and she was chasing the animal round the kitchen with a broom. She had been just about to go out, and had put her hat on her head – a pretty, flowery hat with ribbons.

Just as Dame Tip-Tap finished whispering the magic words, Mrs Doodle's head vanished. It simply wasn't there any more. At least, nobody could see it! Mrs Gobo stared in wonder and amazement. There was Mrs Doodle, quite all right up to her neck. Then there was a space – and then her flowery hat. No head at all.

"What are you staring at, Mrs Gobo?" said Mrs Doodle's voice, most annoyed. "Isn't my hat straight on my head?"

"I don't know," said Mrs Gobo. "You've lost your head! Your hat is there all right – but your head is gone!"

"Stuff and nonsense!" said Mrs Doodle, very sharply indeed. She went to the mirror and gazed into it. But she couldn't see her head, because it had vanished. But there was her flowery hat, neatly perched in the air, going wherever Mrs Doodle went. It was most peculiar.

"Oh, oh, oh!" squealed Mrs Doodle, in a dreadful fright. "Where's my head? Where's it gone?"

"I said you'd lose it one day," said Mrs Gobo, beginning to laugh. "You always lost it over the silliest little

things – and now it really has gone. You shouldn't make such a fuss, Mrs Doodle – then you would keep your head and be sensible, like me and Mrs Twinks."

"I'm going to the doctor," said poor Mrs Doodle, in a greater fright than ever. "I'm going to the doctor."

She rushed out into the street. How people stared to see her coming along without any head at all! Her hat bobbed along perkily, but it didn't seem to be sitting on any head. It was most comical. Everyone laughed loudly. They felt certain that Dame Tip-Tap had used some of her magic, and they enjoyed the joke.

The doctor rubbed his eyes when Mrs Doodle burst into his house. "Who are you?" he said. "Haven't you forgotten something? You seem to have left your head at home."

"Doctor, Doctor, make me better!" begged Mrs Doodle. "Where's my head? It's gone! I know I do lose my head and get into dreadful fusses when things don't happen as I want them to – but, oh, I never never thought my head would vanish like this. Give me some medicine to get it back."

"I can't," said the doctor, watching the flowery hat nodding up and down. "You'll have to go without your head till it comes back of its own accord, Mrs Doodle. Then be careful never to lose it again!"

Mrs Doodle hurried back home, very frightened and miserable. She didn't see Dame Tip-Tap behind her, blowing some purple powder over her hat, whispering magic words all the while. Her head appeared again at once, but she didn't know it. Everyone saw it come back, and most people were rather glad. It was all right to lose your head for a little while, but not for always!

Mrs Doodle went into her bedroom to take off her hat, and goodness, gracious me, there was her head back again under the hat, the eyes staring at her, and tears trickling down the cheeks.

"Oh! I've got my head back!" cried Mrs Doodle in delight. "Mrs Gobo! Mrs Gobo! Mrs Twinks! Dame Tip-Tap! My head's back. It feels fine. It's as firm as can be. I only lost it for a little while. Does it look all right?"

"Quite all right," said Mrs Gobo, coming into the bedroom. "But, Mrs Doodle, yours must be a strange kind of head, if you can lose it as easily as that. It's come back this time all right, but it might not another time. So do be careful, won't you?"

"Oh, yes, I will!" said Mrs Doodle, wiping the tears away. "Oh, I do feel so happy now. Come and have a cup of tea with me, all of you. Do!"

So they did. Mrs Doodle boiled the kettle, and when she went to make the tea she burnt herself on the hot kettle.

"Oh!" she yelled, and danced round the kitchen, squealing. "Oh! You horrid kettle! Why did you do that?"

Everyone watched Mrs Doodle's head as if they expected it to vanish again.

Mrs Doodle remembered, and rushed to the glass to see if it was still there. It was.

"I must be careful," she said, calming down. "I must be very, very careful."

She is. She hardly ever gets into a fuss now. I wish I'd been there when she lost her head. Don't you?

Bing-Bong, the paw-reader

Flip and Binkle had been good for a week and three days, and Binkle was beginning to find things very dull.

"Oh!" he groaned, "can't we find a more exciting job than delivering medicine for Sammy Squirrel the chemist? I hate carrying baskets of bottles every day."

Flip preferred to be good. He was afraid of Binkle's exciting ideas; they nearly always led to trouble.

"It's a *very nice* job," he said anxiously. "For goodness sake don't give it up, Binkle."

Binkle put on his cap and opened the door of their home, Heather Cottage.

"Come on!" he said crossly. "I won't

give up the job – not until we get a better one, anyway!"

The two rabbits ran across Bumble Bee Common on their way to Oak Tree Town. When they got there, Binkle saw a big notice pinned up outside Dilly Duck's at the Post Office. He crossed over to look at it. In big letters it said:

A GRAND BAZAAR
WILL BE HELD IN
OAK TREE TOWN

Binkle stroked his fine whiskers and began thinking.

"Come on," said Flip, pulling him next door into Sammy Squirrel's. "Don't dream like that, Binkle. It's time we began work."

But all that day Binkle went on thinking, and hardly said a single word to Flip. In the evening, when Sammy Squirrel paid him, Binkle gave Flip a dreadful shock.

205

"We shan't be here tomorrow," he said, "so I'm afraid you must get someone else to do the job."

"Oh, Binkle!" cried Flip in dismay. "Whatever do you mean?"

"Sh! I've got a lovely idea!" said Binkle, pulling Flip outside. "Come on, and I'll talk to you about it."

"I don't like your lovely ideas," wailed Flip.

"You'll love this one," said Binkle. "Listen. Did you read that notice about the Bazaar outside Dilly Duck's?"

"Yes," said Flip. "What about it?"

"Well, at the Bazaar there's going to be Bing-Bong, who can read all your life in your paw," said Binkle excitedly. "He'll tell you what's going to happen to you in the future, too."

"Bing-Bong! I never heard of *him*," said Flip. "Anyway, what's it to do with us?"

"Oh, Flip, *can't you guess? One of us will be Bing-Bong*, and read everyone's paws!" said Binkle excitedly.

"Binkle! How can you be so silly?" gasped Flip. "You *know* we can't read paws!"

"Well, we don't need to, silly!" grinned Binkle. "We know all about everyone in Oak Tree Town, don't we? And we can easily tell them all about themselves. They won't know us, for we'll be dressed up, and they'll think we're wonderful!"

"But how can we tell them what will happen in the future?" asked Flip.

"We'll make it up!" said Binkle. "Oh, Flip, what fun it will be!"

"Will it?" said Flip doubtfully. "But look here, Binkle – you're to be Bing-Bong. I don't look a bit like a Bing-Bong person. You do, you're so fat and big, and you've got such lovely whiskers."

Binkle twirled them proudly.

"Yes, I shall be Bing-Bong," he said, "and you can be my assistant. First I must write a note to Herbert Hedgehog, who's putting on the Bazaar."

He sat down and got pen and paper. Presently he showed a letter to Flip. This is what it said:

BING-BONG CASTLE

Dear Sir,

I am Bing-Bong, the reader of paws. I am passing through Oak Tree Town on the day your Bazaar is held. I will call there and read paws.

Yours faithfully,
Bing-Bong.

"There!" said Binkle proudly. "What do you think of that?"

Flip's nose went nervously up and down as he read the letter.

"I *do* hope it will be all right!" he sighed. "You do have such extraordinary ideas, Binkle. I don't know how you think of them."

The letter was sent, and when it reached Herbert Hedgehog he was most excited. He at once arranged to have a little room set apart in Oak Tree Town

Hall for Bing-Bong to sit in and read paws.

"It *will* be grand," he said. "Lots of people will come to the Bazaar now!"

Binkle and Flip were very busy making clothes to wear. Binkle wore a purple suit with a red cloak wound tightly round him. On his head he wore a pointed hat with red stars painted all over it. He looked very grand.

Flip was dressed in baggy trousers and a little black velvet coat. He didn't like them much, for he felt he looked rather silly.

At last the day came, and the two rogues set out over Bumble Bee Common.

"Now remember," said Binkle, "call me Your Highness, and bow before you speak, Flip. You take the money and keep it safe. Leave the rest to me."

Flip wished he could leave *everything* to Binkle, and not go at all, but he didn't dare to say so.

"Oh my! There's Herbert Hedgehog waiting to greet us outside the Town Hall!" he whispered. "Do you think he'll see through our disguise, and know it's us?"

"Of course not!" snapped Binkle, striding forward. Herbert Hedgehog bowed very low when he saw the red-cloaked visitor.

"This is His Royal Highness Bing-Bong!" stammered Flip nervously.

Herbert stood all his prickles up very straight and made way for the two rabbits to go in.

"Very good of you to come, Your Highness," he said, and led the way to the little room at the back of the Hall. "I've made this room ready for you. We shall love to have our paws read by the wonderful Bing-Bong." And he bowed again.

Binkle looked round when Herbert had gone out.

"I'll sit in that big chair," he said. "You stand by the door, Flip. Charge a penny a time, remember."

Very soon there came a timid little knock. Flip swung the door open. Outside stood Creeper Mouse.

"Please, I've come to have my paw read," he said nervously, holding out a penny.

"Your Highness! Someone to have his paw read!" called Flip, beginning to enjoy himself.

Binkle put on some big spectacles and glared at Creeper, who stood tremblingly looking at him. He knew Creeper very well, for he was the postman of Oak Tree Town.

"Come here," commanded Binkle, "and hold out your paw."

Creeper put out his tiny little paw. Binkle stared and stared at it.

"Your paw tells me many things," he said. "It tells me that you have five brothers and sisters. You are married, and you —"

"Oh! oh! oh!" squeaked Creeper, lost in wonder. "How clever you are! It's quite true. Does my paw really tell you that?"

"Of course it does," answered Binkle. "Don't interrupt. It tells me that you walk miles and miles every day carrying a heavy bag."

"Yes, yes, I do," squeaked Creeper. "What's in the bag?"

"Your paw will tell me," said Binkle solemnly, bending closely over it. "Let me see – yes, you carry letters. You are a postman."

"Well, did you ever!" exclaimed the astonished mouse, swinging his tail about delightedly. "Oh, Bing-Bong, please tell me what will happen in my future."

Binkle looked at his paw again. "You will go on a long journey, in a ship," he said gravely. "You will carry letters all your life. You will have twenty-nine children."

"No! no!" shrieked Creeper in horror, snatching his paw away. "Twenty-nine children! Why, how would I feed them all? Oh! oh! Twenty-nine children!"

And he rushed out of the room before Binkle could say another word.

Flip began giggling, but Binkle told him to be quiet.

"*Ssh!*" he said. "Creeper will be telling all the others at the Bazaar, and in a minute they'll all want to come and have their paws read. Listen! There's someone now, Flip."

It was Herbert Hedgehog, holding out his penny and looking rather nervous.

"Creeper Mouse says you're wonderful, Your Highness," he said to Binkle. "Could you read *my* paw, please?"

Binkle looked at it solemnly.

"You live in a yellow cottage," he said. "You grow very fine cabbages."

"So I do – so I do," said Herbert, in the greatest astonishment.

"You have many friends," went on Binkle, "but the two who love you best are –"

"Who?" asked Herbert eagerly,

wondering if they were Dilly Duck and Sammy Squirrel.

"They are – Flip and Binkle Bunny!" said Binkle, now thoroughly enjoying himself.

Flip's nose went up and down in delight, when he saw the astonishment on Herbert's face.

"My best friends!" echoed Herbert. "Flip and Binkle Bunny! Well, well, well! I must be nicer to them in future."

"I *should*," said Binkle, twirling his whiskers very fast, to hide the smile on his face.

"Tell me some more," begged Herbert. "Tell me about the future."

"Er – if you dig up your biggest cabbages, you *may* find a pot of gold underneath," began Binkle.

"Fancy! Oh, my goodness! Oh, excuse me!" begged Herbert, almost stuttering with excitement. "Pray excuse me! I *do* want to go home straight away and see if I can find that gold."

"Oh no, don't do that," shouted Binkle

in alarm . . . but Herbert was gone.

"Bother!" said Binkle in dismay.

"What do you want to go and say such a silly thing for?" demanded Flip in disgust. "You *know* there's no gold under his cabbages."

"*Ssh!* There's someone else," whispered Binkle, as a knock came at the door.

It was Wily Weasel the policeman! Flip almost fell backwards in fright.

"May I have my paw read?" asked Wily politely.

"Oh – er – yes!" stammered Flip, wishing to goodness he could run away.

Wily went up to Binkle and bowed. Binkle took hold of his paw and glared at it. He didn't like Wily Weasel, for Wily had often told him off for being naughty.

"Your paw does not tell me nice things," he began. "It tells me that you are always hunting others and being unkind to them."

"I have to be," said Wily Weasel

cheerfully. "I'm a policeman! There are lots of rogues about Oak Tree Town, and I have to punish them!"

Binkle decided to change the subject. "You are married," he said, "and you love to smoke a pipe."

"Quite right," said Wily, in a pleased voice. "Now tell me about the future. Shall I get rich?"

"*Never!*" said Binkle firmly. "You'll get poorer and poorer. You'll lose your job. You'll be hunted away from Oak Tree Town. You'll be put in prison. You'll –"

"Ow!" yelled Wily in terror, as he listened to all the awful things Binkle was telling. "Don't tell me any more! I don't want to hear anything else!"

He went hurriedly out of the room, groaning and sighing.

"Ooh, I *did* enjoy that," said Binkle. "That's made up for a good deal of trouble I've had from Wily."

Thick and fast came the knocks on the door, and Binkle was as busy as could be, telling everyone about themselves. As he knew all their pasts and made up their futures, he enjoyed himself thoroughly – till in walked someone he *didn't* know!

He was a badger. He held out his paw to Binkle and waited.

"Er – er – er –" began Binkle. "You live far away from here."

"No, I don't," said the Badger. "I live in the next town."

"That's what I meant," cried Binkle. "Er – er – you are married."

"I'm not!" said the badger indignantly. "You don't know what you're talking about! You're a fraud!"

Just at that moment there came a great hubbub outside the door and it burst open suddenly. Herbert Hedgehog came stamping in, followed by a whole crowd of others.

"I've pulled up all the lovely cabbages in my garden," he wailed, "and there's not a piece of gold anywhere! And all my beautiful cabbages are wasted! You're a fraud, Bing-Bong — that's what you are!"

"Yes, he is," cried the badger. "Why, he told me I was married, and I'm not!"

Wily Weasel strode up to Bing-Bong and glared at him.

"Are you Bing-Bong, or aren't you?" he demanded. "Were all those awful things true that you said were going to happen to me — or not?"

"Oh! oh!" wept Flip. "They weren't true, Wily; he made them up, truly he did!"

Wily turned round and looked at Flip. He grabbed off his queer-shaped hat and the green muffler that hid his chin.

"Oho!" he said, "so it's Flip Bunny, is it? And I suppose Bing-Bong is our old friend Binkle?"

Binkle decided to make the best of it.

"Yes," he said, "I'm Binkle. I only came to the Bazaar to give you a bit of fun. I'm sorry about your cabbages, Herbert. Flip, give him the pennies you've got. He can buy some more."

Everyone stared in astonishment at the red-cloaked rabbit. They could hardly believe it was Binkle who had read their paws. They had so believed in him. For a minute everyone felt angry and probably Flip and Binkle would have been punished – if Creeper Mouse hadn't begun to laugh.

"He told me I'd have twenty-nine children," he squeaked. "Oh dear! Oh dear! And I believed him!"

Then everyone began laughing, and even Wily Weasel joined in.

"I'll let you off *this* time," he said to Binkle. "But next time – you just look out! Go off home, both of you. Give Herbert your pennies to buy more cabbages – and don't let me hear any more of you for a *long* time!"

Flip and Binkle scampered off to Heather Cottage as fast as they could go, very thankful to get off so easily.

And for two weeks Binkle had no more lovely ideas.

The well-mannered
scarecrow

Now once there was an old scarecrow who stood out in the fields by day and night, and flapped his jacket at all the rooks and jackdaws that came by.

He was a funny old creature. He had a turnip for a head, a scarf round his broomstick neck, an old ragged coat, and one leg. He had two arms made of sticks, and somebody had given him an old hat on his turnip head.

The scarecrow was very proud of this hat. There was a scarecrow in the next field, but he had no hat at all on *his* turnip head. And the one in the field on

the other side hadn't even a head – so the scarecrow felt quite proud to have not only a head, but a hat as well.

One night the brownies came into the field. They were really excited.

"The Queen is coming by this way tonight!" they said. "The Queen! Imagine that! She is so lovely. We will all come into this field, and cheer her and wave our hats."

"See that our brownie children are taught to curtsey, if they are girls, and to take off their hats if they are boys," said the head brownie.

"And even the rabbits must bow," said another brownie. "Good manners are very important. By the way, we must tell the toadstool brownie to be sure to wear his soldier's uniform and salute the Queen properly. He could put out his flag too. That would please her."

The scarecrow listened to all this, and felt quite excited himself.

"Will the Queen come anywhere near

me?" he called. "I'd so like to see her."

"Of course she will come near," said the head brownie. "And you must raise your hat politely to her. Don't forget."

"But I don't know how to raise my hat, and I shan't even know who the Queen is," said the scarecrow in a troubled voice. "My eyes are not awfully good, you know."

"Well, we will teach you how to raise your hat," said the brownies. "And you must do it when you hear us shout: 'Here comes Her Majesty the Queen!' Now, are you ready? You must bend your arm, take your hat off, and then put it back again. Now — one, two, three — here comes the Queen!"

The old scarecrow bent his stick of an arm, took hold of his hat, lifted it from his head — and dropped it on the ground!

"No, no," said the brownies. "That won't do. That really isn't polite, you know. Put your hat back on your *head*. Surely you know where your head is?"

"Well, I can't see it anywhere," said

the scarecrow, looking all round.

"Isn't he silly?" said the brownies to one another. "Of course he can't see his own head! Now, listen, Scarecrow – all you have to do is to put your hat back to where you lift it from. That's where your head is. Now then – one, two, three – here comes the Queen!"

The scarecrow tried again, and this time he managed not only to take off his hat but to put it back again – a little crooked, it is true, but still he managed it! The brownies praised him, and made him practise it again and again.

Well, when the Queen did come by that night, the scarecrow was as proud as could be because he was the only scarecrow who knew how to behave!

"The one over there hasn't a hat, so he can't raise it, and the other scarecrow hasn't even a head, so he doesn't know about the Queen," he thought happily. "This will be the proudest moment of my life."

Well, you should have seen the old

scarecrow when the Queen came by! He couldn't see well enough to make out who she was – but as soon as the brownies shouted, "Here comes the Queen!" his arm went up, he raised his hat very smartly, held it in the air for a moment, and then put it back again.

"What a clever and well-mannered scarecrow!" said the Queen's silvery voice as she passed. The scarecrow almost fell over with pride.

The brownies were pleased with him. "You did very well," they said. "We are proud of you."

Well, the old scarecrow is still standing out in the fields, his hat on his head, dreaming of the wonderful night when he raised that hat to the Queen. And now I am going to tell you a most peculiar thing.

If anyone goes into the field and shouts, "Here comes the Queen!" the scarecrow at once raises his hat most politely, and then puts it neatly back again on his head.

I can't tell you which scarecrow it is, because, as you know, scarecrows haven't names as we have. So if you think it *might* be the scarecrow in the fields near you, you'll know how to find out for certain. Shout out, "Here comes the Queen!" and see what happens.

I *do* hope he takes off his hat to you!

Nobody came to tea

There was once a lonely hare. He hadn't any friends, and he wanted some.

He talked to the scarecrow in the field, and the scarecrow gave him some advice.

"Ask people to tea. They like that. That is what children do. Give a party sometime, and ask all the creatures to come."

It was summer-time when the scarecrow told the hare this. The hare felt excited. "It will take me a long time to get things for the party," he said. "I will ask everyone for the last week in October. Then I shall have plenty of time to collect food for my guests."

He asked the little dormouse, who was delighted. He asked the prickly hedgehog, and he was very pleased. He asked both the frog and the toad, and as they were cousins they said they would come together.

"That's four," said the hare. "Now, who's next to be asked? Oh yes – I'll ask the lizard and the snake, and I'll ask the little black bat too. He will enjoy a party. I must try to get some beetles for him."

So he asked them all, and they said yes, they would all come to tea with him and be friends.

"Seven guests," the hare told the scarecrow. "It's a *real* party, isn't it?"

Well, the day of the party came. The hare had collected food for every one of his guests, and he set it all out in his field.

Then he waited for his visitors to come. But nobody came to tea. Nobody at all. The dormouse didn't turn up, and neither did the hedgehog. The frog and

toad were not to be seen. The lizard didn't come frisking along, and no gliding, silent snake came to tea. Even the little black bat was missing too.

The hare was sad. "Nobody likes me," he said. "Nobody has come to tea. They said they would – but they were making fun of me. They didn't mean to come."

"What's the matter?" said the rabbit, who was passing by. The hare told him. The rabbit laughed loudly.

"Silly hare! The dormouse is down at the bottom of the ivy-roots, asleep. The hedgehog is snoring in a hole in the bank over there. The frog is at the bottom of the pond, and the toad asleep under a stone. The lizard is in a hollow stump, and the snake sleeps with his brothers in an old tree. The little black bat is asleep too, hanging upside down in the barn."

"Asleep! Why are they all asleep?" said the hare.

"Well, they always sleep the winter away – didn't you know that?" said the rabbit scornfully. "It's no good having a party at this time of year. But cheer up – I and my family will come if you like. We shan't eat the tea you've got ready – but we'll all play games."

So they did, and the hare enjoyed himself after all. But none of his real guests came to the party – they wouldn't wake up till the spring-time.

Slowcoach Sammy

Slowcoach Sammy belonged to a family of brownies, and you can guess why he had such a funny name. He *was* such a slowcoach! He was last in everything, and his mother, Mrs Trot-About, got quite cross with him.

"You're always last, Sammy," she said. "I call the others, and they come running at once. But you stay behind and make me feel so cross."

Poor old Slowcoach Sammy! He missed the bus when he went shopping. He missed the train when Mrs Trot-About took the family to see Aunt Twinkle. He even missed the elephant when he went to the zoo, so he couldn't have his ride.

One day his mother called to all her family, "Come with me. I want you to do some gardening. I have lettuce, mustard and cress seeds, and we will plant them all in our garden so that we shall have plenty to eat in the summer."

Tickle came running. Humps rushed up. Jinky came round the corner at top speed. Ricky arrived panting. But Slowcoach Sammy wasn't to be seen, as usual.

"He's watching a spider making its web at the front gate," said Tickle.

"Sammy, Sammy, Sammy! Hurry up or you won't have time to do any gardening!" cried Mrs Trot-About. "I've only twenty minutes to spare to help you all plant your seeds."

But Slowcoach Sammy didn't hurry. He watched the spider till she had finished her web. Then he watched a worm wriggling out of a hole. Then he watched a bird flying right up into the sky. And at last he got to his mother and his brothers and sisters.

But they had finished their gardening and were picking up their spades to put them back into the shed.

"What a slowcoach you are, Sammy!" said Mrs Trot-About. "I called you ages ago! Now we have finished, and all the seeds are planted."

"I want to plant some seeds too," said Sammy.

"Well, you can't. The others have planted them all – there they are, neatly labelled in rows," said his mother, waving her spade to the garden-beds.

"I *do* want to plant some seeds!" wept Sammy. "I want some plants of my own too. I *do* want to plant some seeds!"

"It's no use making that noise," said his mother. "You should have come when you were called. There are no more seeds at all."

Sammy went off to cry in the playroom. He hunted in the cupboard to see if there *were* any packets of seeds left. And at last he came to a little packet that rattled when he shook it.

He opened it. Inside lay a great many tiny coloured round things.

"Seeds!" said Slowcoach Sammy, delighted. "Seeds that everybody else has forgotten. I'll go and plant them straightaway, and won't the others look blue when they see I *have* got seeds coming up after all!"

Well, if Sammy had looked closely at that packet, he would have seen that they were tiny beads belonging to his sister Jinky! But he didn't. He just hurried out to plant them.

He made little holes along his garden-bed and shook the beads inside. He covered them up well. He watered them, and patted down the ground nicely. He was very pleased with himself.

"They can call me Slowcoach all they like, but they'll be surprised when they see how much nicer my seeds are than theirs!" said Sammy to himself. "My word, with seeds coloured as brightly as that I ought to have flowers all colours of the rainbow!"

Well, the other seeds began to come up, showing a green mist in the beds – but Slowcoach Sammy's didn't peep through at all! He went out to look twenty times a day, but it wasn't any use – he didn't see a single green head coming through the soft brown earth.

He was *so* disappointed. The seeds of the others grew and grew – but Sammy's didn't come up at all. (And *I'm* not really surprised, are you?)

Mrs Trot-About was sorry to see Sammy so unhappy about his seeds. He had told her that he had found a forgotten packet in the cupboard, and she thought they were mustard and cress or lettuce. She couldn't *think* why they didn't come up.

"I shall dig them up and see what's the matter with them," said Slowcoach Sammy to the others.

"Maybe they are slowcoaches like you!" said Jinky. They all came with him and watched him dig up his bed.

He turned up heaps of the little round coloured things and picked them out of the earth.

"Just look!" he said. "They haven't put out any root or shoot or bud or leaf! What bad seeds they are!"

Then the others began to laugh. How they laughed! "What's the matter?" asked Sammy, in surprise. "Do you think my seeds are so funny?"

"Yes, we do!" laughed Ricky. "What did you expect to grow from those seeds, Sammy? Necklace flowers and bracelet buds? They are tiny little *beads*!"

Poor Sammy Slowcoach! He stood and stared at his bead-seeds and tears trickled down his red cheeks. No wonder they wouldn't grow! He had planted beads!

"Never mind, Sammy, you can share my lettuces," said kind Jinky.

"It's not the same to share," said Sammy. "I want seeds of my own."

"Then you mustn't be such a little

slowcoach next time," said his mother. "We'll try and help you not to be."

And what do you think his family say to him when they see Sammy being slow? They say, "Hi, Sammy! Your beads will never grow unless you hurry up!"

Then, my goodness, how he hurries and scurries!

Dame Thimble's work

Dame Thimble lived in a little house at the end of Chuckle Village. She was very clever with her needle, and could make the loveliest, frilliest dresses for the little folk that you could imagine.

They all went to her for their party dresses. She used gossamer thread for her cotton, so her stitches could never be seen. She sat in the sun and she stitched and sewed, and sewed and stitched all day long.

One day a pixie was rude to her. "Oho!" thought Dame Thimble, "next time you come to me for a frilly party dress, my dear, I'll sew a nasty little spell inside it, that I will. And you'll get

SUCH a surprise when you wear it!"

So, when the pixie came along and gave an order for a new frilly dress, Dame Thimble sewed away at it busily. She stitched a nasty little spell in it, too.

"This will make the pixie stamp and shout and put out her tongue and behave as rudely as can be!" chuckled the old dame to herself. "Then everyone will be shocked and she will be turned out of the party!"

243

She sent the frilly dress to the pixie. But the pixie didn't want it for herself. Oh no – it was to be a birthday present for her cousin, the little Princess Sylfai! She was to wear it on her birthday.

So, when her birthday came, the Princess Sylfai put on her new frilly dress. Her maid did it up – and then the trouble began!

Sylfai stamped and shouted! She put out her tongue at everyone, and she pinched and punched anyone who came near. The Queen, the King and the maid were upset and distressed.

"She's ill, the poor darling," said the Queen. "She has never behaved like this before. Take off her new dress and pop her into bed, please, Maid."

But, of course, as soon as the dress was off the Princess behaved like her own sweet self again. The Queen stared at the frilly dress. She picked it up and smelt it.

"There's a nasty spell sewn into it!" she cried. "Oh, what a wicked thing to do! Who made this dress?"

"Dame Thimble," said the maid. "Dear, dear, whatever made her do that!"

"Tell her to pack her things and leave Chuckle Village at once," said the Queen. "I won't have her using bad spells like this. My poor little Sylfai – no wonder she behaved so strangely!"

Dame Thimble was full of horror when she heard what had happened. She didn't make any excuses. She packed her things, took her work basket in her arms and left Fairyland by the first bus.

Where did she go to? Well, I've seen some of her handiwork this very day! Yes, some of the lovely delicate frills she makes so well. Shall I tell you where I saw them?

I picked some mushrooms in a field – and under their caps were scores of beautiful frills, with not a stitch in them to be seen. You don't believe me? Well, you look for them yourself then!

Look out for the snowman

Mother Tuppeny was puzzled. She had twelve hens and, quite suddenly, they had almost stopped laying eggs for her.

"They have been laying so well," she said to Mr Peeko next door. "And now they hardly lay at all. What do you think is the matter with them? Shall I give them some medicine, or scold them, or what?"

"No, no," said Mr Peeko. "Your hens look healthy enough, Mother Tuppeny. Perhaps your children have been running in and out, taking the eggs?"

"Oh, no. They always bring them to me when they find any in the nests," said Mother Tuppeny. "It's a great loss,

Mr Peeko – I use such a lot of eggs for the children, you know. I don't know what to give them for breakfast now."

"Now you listen to me, Mother Tuppeny," said Mr Peeko, thinking hard. "I believe a thief may be coming in the night and stealing your eggs. You leave two eggs in one of the nests, and see if they are there the next morning."

So Mother Tuppeny left two eggs in the nest and looked for them the next morning. They were gone! What a shame! She ran crying to Mr Peeko.

"Those two eggs have gone – and there are none at all in the boxes. It's a thief who comes, Mr Peeko. What shall I do?"

"You go to Mr Plod, the policeman, and tell him all about it," said Mr Peeko. "He'll know what to do!"

So Mother Tuppeny went to Mr Plod. He listened gravely, then took out his big black notebook. "Now you listen carefully to me and do exactly as I tell you, Mother Tuppeny," he said. "You go home and tell your children to make a nice big snowman near your hen house, and to leave it there tonight. And if you see me come into your garden when the moon is up, don't take any notice."

So Mother Tuppeny told her children to go and make a fine snowman in her garden by the hen house, and they rushed out in delight.

Soon a great big snowman was built there, with a big round head, a long white body, stones for eyes and buttons, and a twig for his mouth. Mother Tuppeny gave the children one of her old hats and an old shawl to dress him in.

"It's a snow-woman now, not a snowman," cried the children. "Oh, look, Mother, isn't she lovely?"

"Yes, lovely," said Mother Tuppeny, laughing at the funny sight of the old snow-woman with her hat and shawl on. "Now come along in and have tea. It will soon be dark."

They left the snow-woman in the garden and went in to tea. When it got dark Mother Tuppeny thought she heard footsteps in the garden and she guessed it was Mr Plod.

It was. He went down to the hen house and found the snow-woman. He flashed his torch on her and smiled. What a funny-looking creature!

Mr Plod knocked the old snow-woman down so that there was nothing left of her. Then he stood himself in her place, with a white coat over his uniform. He put the old hat on his head, and dragged the red shawl round him. Then he stood quite still.

When the children lifted the curtain and peered out into the moonlight before they went to bed, they laughed.

"Look! There's our old snow-woman out there all alone! How funny she looks!"

"She looks taller than when we built her," said one of the boys.

"But how could she be?" said the other children. "Snow-women don't grow!"

But, of course, theirs *had* grown, because Mr Plod was quite a bit taller than the snow-woman they had built. He stood there very patiently, waiting and waiting.

Nobody came for a long, long time. Then from over the wall at the bottom came a little knobbly figure. Mr Plod tried to see who it was.

"Well, well – it's that nasty mean little Knobbly Goblin!" said Mr Plod to himself. "I've often thought he was up to mischief – and so he is!"

The Knobbly Goblin crept to the hen house. He suddenly saw the snowman – or what he thought was a snowman – and he stopped in fright. Then he laughed a little goblin laugh.

"Ho, ho! You're only a snowman! You thought you could frighten me, standing there, watching. But you can't!"

He went into the hen house and came out with a bag full of eggs. Ha, ha! What a lovely lot!

He went up to the snowman. "Silly old snowman! Wouldn't you like to tell tales of me? But you can't!"

And then, to the Knobbly Goblin's horror, an arm shot out from the snowman and a deep voice said, "You just come along with me!"

He was held tightly in a big hand, and then he was shaken. "Put down those

eggs. You're a thief!" said the snowman.

The Knobbly Goblin was so frightened that he dropped the eggs. Luckily they fell into the snow and didn't break.

"P-p-p-please let me g-g-g-go," he begged. "Snowman, who are you? I've never met a live one before."

Mr Plod didn't answer. He took the

252

goblin to the police station – and there Knobbly saw that it was Mr Plod, the policeman, who had got him. Ooooooh!

Mr Plod went to see Mother Tuppeny the next day. "I've spanked the thief," he told her. "It was that Knobbly Goblin. I've sent him away, and I've made him pay a fine of ten golden pieces to me. Here they are! They will help to pay for all the eggs he has stolen. I was that snowman, Mother Tuppeny!"

"Oh – how I wish I'd seen you all dressed up!" cried Mother Tuppeny. "The children couldn't *think* what had happened to their snow-woman this morning. They were quite sad about her."

"You buy them some sweets," said Mr Plod. "And tell them how I put on the hat and shawl. They won't mind a bit then!"

They didn't, of course. They laughed when they heard about it.

As for Knobbly, he simply can't bear the sight of a snowman now!

Brer Rabbit goes fishing

One winter's night Brer Rabbit thought he would go fishing. He went and called on Brer Terrapin to ask him if he would go too.

"I'm taking my boat," said Brer Rabbit. "I'm going to row right across the river to the other side, to a place where there's plenty of fish. You come, too, Brer Terrapin. We'll catch some good fish for breakfast this hungry weather."

"Do you mind if my old uncle comes, too?" said Brer Terrapin. "Stick your head out, Uncle, and say 'Howdy' to Brer Rabbit."

"Howdy-do!" said Brer Terrapin's old uncle, shooting his neck out suddenly

from under his big shell.

"Howdy!" said Brer Rabbit. "Yes, bring your uncle too, Brer Terrapin. Plenty of room in my boat!"

"Brrrrrr!" said Brer Terrapin as they all three went to find Brer Rabbit's boat tied up by the river. "It's freezing cold, Brer Rabbit. Good thing I've got no whiskers, or they'd freeze up like icicles! You be careful of yours!"

They all got into the boat and Brer Rabbit rowed right across to the other side of the river. "You be careful, Brer Rabbit," said Brer Terrapin, peering over the edge of the boat. "Brer Wolf lives near here, and he likes to fish about here, too. You be careful he doesn't catch you."

Just as he spoke there came a bellow from the bank. It was old Brer Wolf!

"Hey, Brer Rabbit! What are you doing in my bit of fishing-water? You get out!"

Brer Rabbit drew in his oars and threw out a small anchor.

"We'll anchor here," he said to the terrapins, not taking a bit of notice of Brer Wolf's yells. "Don't you worry about all that shouting. It's just noise and nothing else. Brer Wolf's boat has got a hole in it, so he can't come after us. We'll fish here and see what we get."

Well, they caught a whole lot of fish, and Brer Wolf got quite hoarse with shouting at them and telling them to get out of his bit of fishing-water. But pretty soon he got tired of that and went back to his home nearby.

Then Brer Rabbit suddenly noticed that he couldn't jerk his line out of the water. What was happening? He peered over the edge of the boat in the moonlight – and what a shock he got! The river was freezing fast!

"My, my!" said Brer Rabbit, startled. "We'd better get back before the river's quite frozen. It must be a bitter cold night tonight."

But the boat wouldn't move! It was stuck fast in the ice. The oars broke through the ice, but Brer Rabbit couldn't use them. He looked at the terrapins in fright.

"What'll we do? The water's frozen! We're stuck!"

"That's bad," said Brer Terrapin. "See if the ice will hold you, Brer Rabbit. Then maybe we can slide back."

Very soon the ice was hard enough to hold them. But poor Brer Rabbit couldn't go a step without falling down – and as for the terrapins, their legs just slid helplessly on the ice, and they didn't get anywhere at all!

"Brer Wolf will see what's happened when daylight comes!" said Brer Rabbit, with a groan. "He'll put on his skates and skate over the ice to the boat – and maybe he'll have rabbit-and-terrapin pie for his dinner!"

The river was frozen even harder by the morning. Brer Wolf was surprised to see it covered with ice when he peeped out of his window next morning. Aha! There was Brer Rabbit's boat stuck fast in the frozen river.

"Just wait till I get my skates on and I'll catch you all right, Brer Rabbit!" yelled Brer Wolf.

Brer Rabbit watched Brer Wolf come

down to the bank of the frozen river. He watched him put on his skates.

"If only I had some skates!" he groaned. "I'd skate out of sight in two shakes of a duck's tail! But none of us can escape because we can't even *stand* on this slippery ice!"

Then Brer Terrapin's old uncle spoke up. "Maybe I know a way to get us all free," he said. "Now see, Brer Rabbit. Put me out of the boat on to my back – and Brer Terrapin, too."

"What's the use of *that*?" said Brer Rabbit.

"Then after that you get out, too," said Brer Terrapin's uncle. "And you put one foot on my underside and the other on Brer Terrapin's – and we'll catch hold of your toes hard. And you can skate away on us, right to the other side of the river. We'll be your skates, Brer Rabbit; our shells will slide as fast as anything!"

What an idea! Brer Rabbit dropped them on to the ice, upside down, side by side. He hopped overboard himself and put a hind foot on each. The terrapins held his feet firmly in their clawed feet.

Just as Brer Wolf came skating over the ice, Brer Rabbit skated off, too, with the two upside-down terrapins for his skates! He went like the wind – and Brer Wolf was so astonished that his feet caught in one another and over he went, higgledy-piggledy, on the ice.

"Take a few lessons, Brer Wolf, take a few lessons!" yelled out Brer Rabbit, and came to a stop at the opposite bank. The terrapins let go his feet and he leapt off. He put them the right way up, and they scrambled down the nearest hole.

"Like one of my fish, Brer Wolf?" shouted Brer Rabbit, and threw one at Brer Wolf. It hit him smack on the nose – and off went wicked Brer Rabbit with his string of fish, laughing fit to kill himself. And I guess that he and the two terrapins feasted on a fine fish-pie that night!

Peter's good idea

Four children met to play each day by the village pond. They were town children, sent to stay in the country for a long holiday – and what fun they had in the fields and woods!

Peter, Jane, Tom and Bessie knew all the farm animals now. They called the horses by their names; they knew Daisy, Buttercup, Blossom and Sorrel, the prettiest cows in the field. They had been chased by Snorter the bull, so they knew him very well indeed!

They had fed the chickens and ducks; they had watched the piglets grow into fat pigs. They counted the sheep in the fields to make sure none had got out through the hedge, and they loved the tiny kids belonging to the nanny-goat on the common.

They helped to pick the plums and the apples – but now winter was coming on, and there was no more fruit to pick. The blackberries were gone. The nut trees were bare of nuts and of leaves too. There was ice on the village pond.

"I wonder if it will bear us yet," said Jane, and she tried the ice with her foot. It broke at once.

A voice shouted to them, "Now then, children, don't you be silly enough to try that ice yet! It won't be strong enough to bear you till the turn of the year!"

"I wish we had something to do," said Tom. "There's nothing to pick now. No young animals to feed. They won't let us milk the cows or clean out the sheds."

"Well, we'll be able to go sliding after Christmas perhaps," said Jane. So they waited patiently for the frost to harden the ice – but instead of the weather getting colder after Christmas, it became warmer.

"What shall we do today?" said Peter, kicking at a stone. "It's too muddy to go walking. I got my boots so covered with clay yesterday that it took me an hour to clean them this morning."

"Let's go exploring in the lofts," said Bessie. "There's nobody to say we mustn't today. The farmer has gone to market, and his wife is ill in bed."

"Well, we mustn't get into mischief," said Peter, who was the eldest. "We'll only just explore, see?"

So off they all went to explore the lofts whose dusty windows showed here and there at the top of the outbuildings.

It was exciting climbing up the rickety ladders. Some of the lofts were full of rubbish and sacks. It was fun to play hide-and-seek there. One loft was stacked with sacks of different kinds of grain. The old tabby-cat lay on an empty sack up there, purring.

"She's the guardian of the sacks!" cried Jane. "She hunts the mice that come up here. Oh, look – here's a whole nest of tabby kittens in the corner!"

That was a lovely find! The kittens all had their eyes open, and were playful. The tabby-cat let the children play with her kittens for a little while, and then she curled herself round them.

"She thinks they are tired and have had enough of us!" cried Bessie. "Well – we'll leave you alone then, Tabby! Come on – let's go and see what's in the biggest loft of all!"

Down the ladder they went, and ran to the oldest barn. They could find no ladder up to the loft there. They sniffed and sniffed, because there was a lovely smell in that loft.

"I guess the farmer has hidden the ladder," said Tom. "Maybe he doesn't want anyone to go up into this loft."

"Well, we'd better not, then," said Peter.

But the others felt as if they simply *must* explore that loft too. "We'll see if we can find a ladder," said Tom.

"I'm going off to look at the pigs," said

Peter. "I don't think we ought to go up in this loft."

He went off. The others looked after him, and half thought they would follow. But Tom couldn't bear to leave the loft unexplored. He *must* see what that lovely smell was!

The three children hunted about for a ladder. At last they found one. It was long and heavy, but they just managed to carry it between them. They got it into the barn and put it up to the loft. Then up they went, one after another.

"I say! It's the apple-loft!" cried Tom in delight. "Gosh! What a lot of apples!"

"We helped to pick them, didn't we?" said Bessie, sniffing the lovely apple-smell. "Look at those red ones — they came off the big tree by the wall."

"And those green ones came off the little trees, and the brown ones off the trees by the pig-sty," said Tom. "I say — I do feel hungry!"

So did they all, quite suddenly, as they looked at those delicious apples.

The smell got inside them and made them long to dig their teeth into the sweet, juicy apples!

"Let's take some," said Tom. "There are so many that the farmer will never know."

"But we oughtn't to," said Bessie.

"I can't help it!" said Tom. "I just feel I must!"

He picked up an apple – but it was bad on the other side, so he threw it down. He picked up another. That was half bad too.

"These bad apples are making all the others rotten too," said Bessie. "They will soon all be bad – so we'd better eat them whilst they are good!"

"We could creep up here every day and help ourselves to apples!" said Jane, who loved apples.

"Let's take one to Peter," said Tom. So he picked out a fat, red, juicy one, and put it into his pocket for Peter. Then the children climbed down the ladder and went to find him. He was by the pigs.

He liked the pigs – they were always so cheerful and friendly.

"Peter, that loft is *full* of apples!" said Tom. "We've brought one for you. Isn't it a beauty?"

"Tom! You can't do that! They are not your apples!" cried Peter.

"But, Peter, they are all going bad," said Tom crossly. "We may as well eat them whilst they are good. It's such a waste to let things go bad."

"I wonder if the farmer knows his apples are going bad," said Peter. "It's funny he lets them do that. Tom, take these apples back. Bad or good, they are not ours to take."

Tom was sulky. He didn't want to do as Peter told him. It was too bad, just when they had all thought they could munch juicy apples. But Peter glared at him so hard that Tom knew he had better obey. So he took the apples and ran back to the barn, grumbling hard to himself.

"I'll get some apples when Peter isn't

about," said Tom to himself. He threw the apples into the loft and came down again – just in time to see the farmer coming home from market!

How glad Tom was that he and the others were not eating the apples then! He went red, and wondered if the farmer would guess what he had been doing.

The farmer came over to the pigs and looked at them. Peter spoke to him. "Do pigs like rotten apples, sir?" he asked.

"Yes – they'll gobble them all up!" said the farmer. "Why, Peter?"

"Well, sir, did you know that half your apples are going bad up in the loft there?" said Peter. "They'll be turning the good ones rotten, won't they – and that's a pity."

"You're right, Peter," said the farmer. "My wife usually sees to all those jobs for me – the apples quite slipped my mind! Since she's been in bed there's been a lot of jobs left undone – and that's one. All those apples should be sorted out, and gone over every week. The rotten ones should be thrown to the pigs. Dear, dear – what a pity my wife's ill. And it doesn't help her, having to worry about all her jobs."

"*We* could do that job for you!" said Peter at once. "We could sort all the apples every week, sir. Shall we do it?"

"That would be very good of you, Peter," said the farmer. "Yes – that would certainly be a help. Get the others to give you a hand, too. Could you do it today?"

"Of course!" said Peter. He beckoned to the other three. They came up, wondering if the farmer was going to give them a scolding for going into the loft.

They were excited when Peter told them the job they were to do. It would be fun to do that, even if Peter wouldn't let them eat any of the apples! They rushed back to the barn.

"Now, Jane and I will go up the ladder and sort out the apples," said Peter.

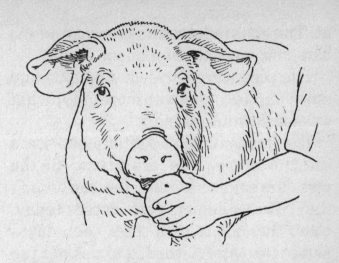

"Tom, you and Bessie must be down here and pick up all the bad ones we throw down. You can put them into the big wheelbarrow and take them to the pigs."

So Peter and Jane were soon very busy indeed sorting out the bad and good apples. Every rotten apple was thrown down to the barn below. Tom and Bessie picked them up busily, and piled them into the barrow.

It was hard work. There were hundreds of apples, all neatly set out on the floor, and every one had to be looked at. The good ones were set back, and the bad ones were thrown down.

The pigs were thrilled. Apples – and more apples – and yet more. My, what a feast for hungry pigs!

The farmer came up after a bit. "Let's see the apples you are giving to the pigs," he said. "My, they *are* bad, aren't they! That's enough for the pigs today. Keep the rest to give them each day – and come every Saturday to sort out the apples again for me. That's a good job you can do, and I shall be very grateful, and so will my wife. It will help to stop her worrying."

"We'll come along, sir," said Peter, scrambling down the ladder. "And you may be sure we shan't eat any of your apples ourselves. I'll see to that!"

"Good boy!" said the farmer. "But, my lad, you must have a little reward for your good idea! You and your friends can help yourselves to a couple of apples each, every day. There are enough apples there to feed an army, if they are well sorted out into good and bad – so you help yourselves, and choose the juiciest you can find! Children that are honest and can be trusted deserve to have a reward!"

"Oh, thank you, sir!" cried Peter in delight. "Two apples a day for each of us – that's lovely."

The kind old farmer went off to his horses. Peter looked at the others. They had gone rather red.

"Yes – I don't wonder you feel a bit ashamed!" said Peter. "You were going to take the apples without permission! And now see what's happened – we've done a good job of work, the farmer is pleased, the farmer's wife will be pleased, the pigs are pleased, and we've got permission to take more apples than we would ever have dared to eat! What do you think of that?"

"We think you had a very good idea, Peter!" said Tom. "And next time we'll have good ideas, too! Now let's eat our apples – aren't they DELICIOUS!"

Betsy-May and the giant-boy

Once a little boy called Harry came
to live next door to Betsy-May. She
heard him shouting to his dog on the
other side of the wall, and she wondered
what he was like.

"I can't see him because the wall is so
high, higher than Daddy's head, even,"
thought Betsy-May. "But perhaps I
could shout to him."

So she shouted to him: "Boy-over-the-
wall! What are you like?"

There was a silence. Then Harry's
voice came over the wall. "I'm a big
giant-boy! Shall I look over the wall at
you?"

"Don't be silly," shouted back Betsy-
May. "There aren't any giant-boys."

"Well, you just see me peeping over!" said Harry. Now Harry had a pair of stilts, and he could walk on them cleverly. When he walked on them they raised him up high, and made him very tall. He ran to get his stilts, climbed up on them and walked to the wall.

And to Betsy-May's enormous surprise, there was Harry's head suddenly looking over the top of the wall at her!

"You're standing on a ladder," she said.

"No, I'm not," said Harry. "Really I'm not. Look – I'll walk down the garden, just against the wall, and you'll see my head bobbing just above the wall all the time. I tell you, I'm a giant-boy!"

Betsy-May watched. Sure enough, as Harry walked down the garden near the wall, perched on his high stilts, she saw his head bob-bobbing over it, just as if he really were a giant-boy on the other side! It was most surprising.

Betsy-May didn't like it. Harry called to her. "Well – I *am* a giant-boy, you see! Wouldn't you like to come and play with me? People don't often have the chance of playing with giant-boys."

"I don't want to play with you," said Betsy-May. "I am sure I couldn't like giant-boys. You would be taller even than my daddy and I shouldn't like it."

"Baby-girl, baby-girl!" cried Harry, looking over the top of the wall again.

Betsy-May gave a squeal and ran off. She wouldn't go near the wall again, but played with Baby James all the morning at the bottom of the garden. Mummy thought she was a very good girl indeed!

The next day Mummy said to Betsy-May: "Darling, Mrs Toms, who lives next door, has a nice boy called Harry. They want you to go there to tea today. As it is only next door, you can go by yourself. It is time you went out to tea alone now."

"I don't want to go," said Betsy-May,

making up her mind that she would never, never go to tea with any giant-boy taller than her own daddy.

"Don't be silly, Betsy-May," said Mummy, quite crossly. "You love going out to tea, and Harry is a very nice little boy."

"He isn't," said Betsy-May. "He's a horrid big boy."

"Betsy-May! Why, you haven't even seen him!" cried her mother.

"Yes, I have. When he walked down the garden, I saw his head bob-bobbing over the top of the wall," said Betsy-May. "He's a giant-boy."

"Betsy-May, now surely you aren't beginning to tell me stories," said her mother, looking very solemn. "I am sure you have never seen Harry – and as for seeing his head bob-bobbing over the wall, well, that is quite impossible."

"I don't want to go to tea with him, all the same," said Betsy-May.

"Well, I'll go with you and take Baby James, too," said Mummy. "I know

Baby James won't be frightened of a nice little boy like Harry."

Betsy-May looked at Mummy. It would be all right if she went too. So she nodded her head and said: "All right – I'll go, but you must keep hold of my hand. I don't like giant-boys at all."

Well, they went to tea that afternoon. Betsy-May couldn't help feeling rather afraid, so she held on to Mummy's hand very tightly. They went into the garden to have tea there – and, dear me, Harry seemed to be only a little boy after all, hardly any bigger than Betsy-May herself.

"You're not a giant-boy after all," said Betsy-May. "I nearly didn't come to tea with you because I don't like giant-boys."

"Shall I show you how I make myself into a giant-boy?" said Harry with a naughty giggle. "Then, if you like, you can try to make yourself into a giant-girl."

Although Betsy-May didn't at all like

giant-boys, she felt it would be most exciting to make herself into a giant-girl. So she nodded her head.

"I'd like to be a giant-girl," she said. "Baby James *would* be surprised."

Harry ran off to get his tall stilts. In a minute he came back, walking on them. They made him very tall, of course. Betsy-May stared in surprise.

"Oh! You've got stilts! You're not really a giant-boy after all! You just walked on those down the garden, and that's how I saw your head over the wall!"

"Of course, silly," said Harry. "Now you try them."

It looked very easy to walk on the stilts because Harry did it so well. But Betsy-May fell off at once. Baby James laughed and gurgled to see her. She tried again and again, and at last managed to walk a few steps. She did feel tall and grand!

Harry and Betsy-May had a fine time together, and Betsy-May was sorry when she had to go home.

"Well, will you go to tea with Harry another time all by yourself?" asked Mummy, as they went home. "Or are you still afraid of him? Such nonsense, saying he was a giant-boy!"

"One day, when you look up, you'll see a giant-*girl* peeping over the next-door wall at you," said Betsy-May. "You just wait, Mummy. You'll get a dreadful fright."

"Well, well, we'll see!" said Mummy, with a laugh. "You just try, and see what happens, Betsy-May."

So Betsy-May goes to play every day with Harry now, and is trying her very hardest to be a giant-girl on his stilts. How surprised everyone will be when she looks over the wall at them!

Tale of a teddy and a mouse

T he new teddy bear was very small indeed. The toys stared at him when he first came into the playroom, wondering what he was.

"Good gracious, I believe you're a teddy bear!" said Amelia Jane, the naughty doll. "I thought you were a peculiar-shaped mouse."

"Well, I'm not," said the small bear sharply, and he pressed himself in the middle. "*Grrrrr*! Hear my growl? Well, no mouse can growl, it can only squeak."

"Yes. You're a bear all right," said the pink rabbit. "I hear you've come to live with us. Well, I'll show you your place in the toy cupboard, right at the back."

"I don't like being at the back, it's too dark," said the little bear. "I'll be at the front here, by this big brick-box."

"Oh, no, you won't. That's *my* place when I want to sit in the toy cupboard," said Amelia Jane. "And let me tell you this, small bear, if you live with us, you'll have to take on lots of little bits of work. We all do. You'll have

to wind up the clockwork clown when he runs down, you'll have to clean the dolls' house windows, and you'll have to help the engine-driver polish his big red train."

"Dear me, I don't think I want to do any of those things," said the bear. "I'm lazy. I don't like working."

"Well, you'll just have to," said Amelia Jane. "Otherwise you won't get any of the biscuit crumbs that the children drop on the floor, you won't get any of the sweets in the toy sweet shop – and we're allowed some every week – and you won't come to any parties."

"Pooh!" said the bear and stalked off to pick up some beads out of the bead-box and thread himself a necklace.

"He's vain as well as lazy," said the rabbit in disgust. "Hey, Bear, what's your name? Or are you too lazy to have one?"

"My name is Sidney Gordon Eustace," said the bear, haughtily. "And I don't like being called Sid."

"Sid!" yelled all the toys at once, and the bear looked furious. He turned his head away, and went on threading the beads.

"Sidney Gordon Eustace!" said the clown, with a laugh. "I guess he gave himself those names. No sensible child would ever call a teddy bear that. Huh!"

The bear was not much use in the playroom. He just would *not* do any of the jobs there at all. He went surprisingly deaf when anyone called to him to come and clean or polish or sweep. He would pretend to be asleep, or just walk about humming a little tune as if nobody was calling his name at all. It was most annoying.

"Sidney! Come and shake the mats for the dolls' house dolls!" the pink rabbit called. No answer from Sidney at all.

"SIDNEY, come here! You're not as deaf as all that."

The bear never even turned his head. "Hey, Sidney Gordon Eustace, come and

285

do your jobs," yelled the rabbit.

No answer.

"All right!" shouted the rabbit, angrily, "you shan't have that nice big crumb of chocolate biscuit we found under the table this morning."

It was always the same whenever there was a job to be done. "Sidney, come here!"

But Sidney never came. He never did one single thing for any of the toys.

"What are we going to do about him?" said the big teddy bear. "I'd like to spank him – but he's too quick for me. Amelia Jane, can't you think of a good idea?"

"Oh, yes," said Amelia at once. "I know what we'll do. We'll get Sidney the mouse to come and do the things that Sidney the bear should do – and he shall have all the crumbs and titbits that the bear should have. He won't like that – a common little house-mouse getting all his treats!"

"Dear me, is the house-mouse's name

Sidney, too?" asked the rabbit in surprise. "I never knew that before. When we want him we usually go to his hole and shout 'Mouse', and he comes."

"Well, I'll go and shout 'Sidney'," said Amelia Jane, "and you'll see – he'll come!" So she went to the little hole at the bottom of the wall near the bookcase and shouted down it.

"Sidney! Sid-Sid-Sidney! We want you."

The little bear, of course, didn't turn round – *he* wasn't going to come when his name was called. But someone very small came scampering up the passage to the entrance of the hole.

It was the tiny brown house-mouse, with bright black eyes and twitching whiskers.

"Ah, Sidney," said Amelia Jane. "Will you just come and shake the mats in the dolls' house, please? They are very dusty. We'll give you a big chocolate biscuit crumb and a drink of lemonade out of the little teapot if you will."

"Can I drink out of the spout?" said the tiny mouse, pleased. "I like drinking out of the spout."

"Yes, of course," said Amelia Jane.

The little mouse set about shaking the mats vigorously, and the job was soon done.

"Isn't Sidney wonderful?" said Amelia in a loud voice to the others. "Sidney the mouse, I mean, of course, not silly Sidney the bear. He wouldn't have the strength to shake mats like that, poor thing. Sidney, here's your chocolate biscuit crumb and there's the teapot full of lemonade."

Sidney the bear didn't like this at all. Fancy making a fuss of a silly little mouse, and giving him treats like that. He would very much have liked the crumb and the lemonade himself.

He pressed himself in the middle and growled furiously when the mouse had gone.

"Don't have that mouse here again," he said. "I don't like hearing somebody else being called Sidney. Anyway, I don't believe his name *is* Sidney. It's not a name for a mouse."

"Well, for all you know, his name might be Sidney Gordon Eustace just like yours," said Amelia Jane at once.

"Pooh! Whoever heard of a mouse having a grand name like that?" said the bear.

"Well, next time you won't do a job, we'll call all three names down the hole," said Amelia, "and see if the little mouse will answer to them!"

Next night there was going to be a party. Everyone had to help to get ready for it. Amelia Jane called to the little bear.

"Sidney, come and set the tables for the party. Sidney, do you hear me?"

Sidney did, but he pretended not to, of course. He wouldn't set party tables! So he went deaf again, and didn't even turn his head.

"Sidney Gordon Eustace, do as you're told or you won't come to the party," bawled the big teddy bear in a rage.

The little bear didn't answer.

Amelia Jane gave a sudden grin. "Never mind," she said. "We'll get Sidney Gordon Eustace, the little mouse, to come and set the tables. He does them beautifully and never breaks a thing. He can come to the party afterwards. I'll call him."

The little bear turned his head. "He won't answer to *that* name, you know he won't!" he said, scornfully. "Call away! No mouse ever had a name as grand as mine."

Amelia Jane went to the mouse-hole and called down it. "Sidney Gordon Eustace, are you there?" she called. "If you are at home, come up and help us. Sidney Gordon Eustace, are you there?"

And at once there came the pattering of tiny feet and, with a loud squeak, the little mouse peeped out of his hole, his whiskers quivering.

"Ah – you are at home," said Amelia. "Well, dear little Sidney, will you set the tables for us? We're going to have a party!"

The mouse was delighted. He was soon at work, and in a short while the four tables were set with tiny tablecloths and china. Then he went to help the dolls' house dolls to cut sandwiches.

The little bear watched all this out of the corner of his eye. He was quite amazed that the mouse had come when he was called Sidney Gordon Eustace – goodness, fancy a common little mouse owning a name like that!

He was very cross when he saw that the mouse was going to the party. Amelia Jane found him a red ribbon to tie round his neck and one for his long tail. He was given a place at the biggest table, and everyone made a fuss of him.

"Good little Sidney! You do work well! Whatever should we do without you? What will you have to eat?"

The mouse ate a lot. Much too much,

the little bear thought. *He* didn't go to the party. He hadn't been asked and he didn't quite like to go because there was no chair for him and no plate. But, oh, all those nice things to eat! *Why* hadn't he been sensible and gone to set the tables?

"Goodnight, Sidney Gordon Eustace," said Amelia to the delighted mouse. "We've loved having you."

After this kind of thing had happened three or four times the bear got tired of it. He hated hearing people yell for "Sidney, Sidney!" down the mouse-hole or hearing the mouse addressed as Sidney Gordon Eustace. It was really too bad. Also, the mouse was getting all the titbits and the treats. The bear didn't like that either.

So the next time that there was a job to be done, the bear decided to do it. He suddenly heard the rabbit say, "Hello! The big red engine is very smeary. It wants a polish again. I'll go and call Sidney."

The pink rabbit went to the mouse-hole and began to call down it. "Sidney, Sidney, Sidney!"

But before the mouse could answer, Sidney the bear rushed up to the rabbit. "Yes! Did you call me? What do you want me to do?"

"Dear me, you're not as deaf as usual," said the rabbit, surprised. "Well, go and polish the red engine, then. You can have a sweet out of the toy sweet shop if you do it properly."

Sidney did do it properly.

The pink rabbit came and looked at the engine and so did Amelia Jane.

"Very nice," said Amelia. "Give him a big sweet, Rabbit."

The bear was pleased. He had done the mouse out of a job. The toys had been pleased with him, and the sweet was delicious.

And after that, you should have seen Sidney the bear rush up whenever his name was called. "Yes, yes – here I am. What do you want me to do?"

Very soon the little mouse was not called up the hole any more and Sidney the bear worked hard and was friendly and sensible.

The toys began to like him, and Sidney liked them, too.

But one thing puzzled the rabbit and the big teddy bear, and they asked Amelia Jane about it.

"Amelia Jane – how did you know that the mouse's name was Sidney Gordon Eustace?"

"It isn't," said Amelia with a grin.

"But it must be," said the rabbit. "He always came when you called him by it."

"I know – but he'd come if you called *any* name down his hole," said Amelia. "Go and call what name you like – he'll come! It's the calling he answers, not the name. He doesn't even know what names are."

"Good gracious!" said the rabbit and the bear, and they went to the mouse-hole.

"William," called Rabbit, and up came the mouse. He was given a crumb and went down again.

"Polly-Wolly-Doodle," shouted the big bear, and up came the mouse for another crumb.

"Boot-polish," shouted Rabbit, and up came the mouse.

"Tomato soup," cried the big bear.

It didn't matter what name was shouted down the hole, the mouse always came up. He came because he heard a loud shout, that was all.

Amelia Jane went into fits of laughter when the mouse came up at different calls. Penny stamp! Cough-drop! Sid-Sid-Sid! Dickory-Dock! Rub-a-dub-dub!

The mouse's nose appeared at the hole each time. How the toys laughed – all except Sidney the bear!

He didn't laugh. He felt very silly indeed. Oh, dear, what a trick Amelia Jane had played on him. But suddenly he began to laugh, too. "It's funny," he cried. "It's funny!"

In the King's shoes

Once upon a time the brownie pedlar Twiddles was sitting down by the lane-side mending a kettle. As he sat there, who should come along but the King of Brownie Land himself! He was walking slowly, as if he were tired. He saw Twiddles sitting by the lane-side and he sat down by him.

"Your Majesty, can I run to the nearest cottage and get a chair for you?" said Twiddles, jumping up and bowing.

"No," said the King. "Let me sit in the grass for once if I wish to. My shoes hurt me. I shall take them off for a few minutes while I talk to you."

The King slipped off his beautiful,

highly polished shoes with their silver laces.

"My word!" said Twiddles the pedlar. "I'd dearly love to be in your shoes for a little while, Your Majesty."

"You would, would you?" said the King. "Well, it's a silly, foolish wish of yours, but I'll grant it! Get into my shoes – and you'll find yourself King! I'll be a pedlar for a few happy hours!"

Hardly believing his ears, Twiddles got into the King's shoes. They fitted him perfectly. He stood up and gazed down at himself in astonishment. He was dressed like a king – and the King was dressed like a pedlar! Such was the magic in the King's shoes! Whoever wore them could be the King himself!

"Go down the lane and you'll meet my servants," said the King. "Good luck to you! I'm going to have a snooze in the shade here and listen to the birds singing."

Twiddles went down the lane, holding his head high, and looking as proud

as could be. He was King! King! How grand it felt!

He saw some men hurrying towards him.

"Your Majesty, Your Majesty!" they cried. "You will be late for the opening of that sale of work. Hurry, Sire!"

"Dear me," thought Twiddles, "so I am to open a sale of work, and everyone will bow to me and cheer me. How fine!"

He hurried to a waiting carriage and climbed into it. He drove off quickly to the next town. How the people there cheered him! He opened the sale of work, and read a speech that was put before him. He stood in the hot sun for about an hour, shaking hands with all kinds of brownies. He began to feel tired.

"I say, isn't it about time for dinner?" he asked a courtier nearby.

"Not nearly," said the brownie, looking surprised. "You have to review your troops of Scouts next, Your Majesty. Have you forgotten?"

"Oh, well," thought Twiddles, "it will be fun to ask the Scouts all about their camp fires and the best way to boil kettles on them. I am sure I could teach them a thing or two about that!"

But, to his surprise, when he began to talk to the Scouts about this sort of thing his courtiers nudged his arm and frowned.

"Your Majesty is not supposed to know how kettles are boiled or camp fires made!" they whispered. "Those are not the things a king is interested in."

"Dear me!" thought Twiddles. "How dull it must be to be a king all one's life! How hungry I am getting! Whenever are we going to have dinner? I guess it will be a fine one, with lots of marvellous things to eat and drink!"

But, to his great disgust, as soon as he had finished with the Scouts he was hustled into his carriage and driven off to see a new ship being launched – and a footman presented him with a little packet of sandwiches to eat!

"Is this all my dinner?" asked poor Twiddles. "Just sardine sandwiches? Well, well, well! I'd be better off if I were a pedlar! I'd at least fry myself bacon and eggs, with an apple or two to follow!"

"Your Majesty, there is no time for you to have a proper lunch today," said the courtier who was with him. "You have to be at the dockyards in half an hour. And after that you have to visit a hospital. And then there is the flower show to go to."

"Do you mean to say that all these things are on one day?" asked Twiddles in disgust. "Don't I get any time off at all?"

"Your Majesty is acting very strangely today," said the courtier, looking troubled. "You promised to do all these things – and a king must keep his promise."

Twiddles launched the new ship. He rushed off to the hospital, and walked round and round the wards, and spoke to everyone in the beds there. By the time he had finished his feet felt as if they could not walk another step, and his face was stiff with smiling so much. He badly wanted a cup of tea.

But no! He had to go to the flower show next, and miss out his tea altogether! He was still very hungry, as he had only had the sandwiches for dinner.

He yawned and yawned at the flower show, and his courtiers looked most disgusted with him. He didn't at all want to see the beautiful flowers they showed him. He didn't want to smell any of them. He just wanted to sit down on a chair and have a cup of tea all by himself.

When the flower show was over he was driven to the palace.

Twiddles was thrilled to see it shining in the evening sun. The people cheered him as he passed. Twiddles forgot about his dull and tiring day and waved his hat to the people. But that was not the thing to do at all. He had to bow stiffly from left to right and from right to left. He got out of the carriage and went up the long flight of steps.

"I want a jolly good meal now," he said to the courtiers.

They looked surprised. "Your Majesty, you will only just have time to change into your best uniform and get ready for the big military dinner you are giving tonight," they said.

"Oh, well," thought Twiddles, "I shall certainly have something to eat at the dinner – and I shall look very handsome in a uniform, too."

The uniform was tight and stiff. It cut him round the legs. It cut him across the shoulders. It was heavy. But still, he did look very handsome indeed. He went down to the dinner.

But before he could sit down he found that he had to shake hands with two hundred guests! Twiddles was not used to shaking hands with so many people and his hand soon ached terribly. At last he sat down to the table.

He had a famous general on one side, and a famous prince on the other. They both talked so much that Twiddles hardly had time to eat anything, because he had to keep saying, "Yes, certainly," and, "No, of course not!" almost every moment.

The dinner took a long, long time. Twiddles got very bored. He thought the general and the prince were both very silly. He wished they would stop talking for just one minute. But they didn't.

At last bedtime came. Twiddles felt as if he was being squeezed to death in his tight uniform. He could hardly breathe. He was so very, very glad to get out of it. His servants left him when he was ready for bed. He stood and looked at the beautiful bed ready for him – and he shook his head.

"No," said Twiddles. "I don't want to sleep in you – and wake up in the morning to rush about all day long doing things I don't want to do. It's a difficult thing to be a king. I'd rather be a pedlar. I'm free, but a king is not. A king has many masters and must do as he is told all day long – a pedlar has no master and is as free as the air! I'm going back to be a pedlar again!"

He slipped out of the palace in his sleeping-suit. He made his way to the stables. He jumped on a horse, and rode bareback to the lane-side where he had left the King.

There was a small light there – the remains of a camp fire. A man was sleeping peacefully beside it. It was the real King!

Twiddles woke him. "Wake up!" he said. "I've come back. I'm not a good king! I got hungry and bored. I'd rather be a pedlar."

The King sat up and stared at him.

"Well, I got hungry and bored, too, when I was a king," he said. "I like being a pedlar. It's lovely! Just do what you like, and nobody to say, 'It's your duty to do this or that!' No, Twiddles, you go on being a king. I don't want to go back."

Twiddles kicked off the King's shoes. He had put them on to come back in. In a trice he had changed once again to the untidy pedlar he had been that morning. Even his beautiful sleeping-suit disappeared and he was dressed in his same old clothes. But the King was dressed in the fine sleeping-suit — he was no longer a pedlar!

The King got up. "Well, well," he said, "I suppose I had better go back. After all, it's my job. I must do it as well as I can for the sake of my people, who love me. But oh, Pedlar, you can't think how I have enjoyed today!"

"Yes, I can," said Twiddles, patting the King kindly on the back. "You've enjoyed today just as much as *I* shall enjoy tomorrow. Now, goodnight, Your Majesty, and pleasant dreams!"

Twiddles lay down by the fire. The King galloped back to the palace on the horse. And when the pedlar awoke next morning he wasn't at all sure that it was nothing but a dream!

"Poor old King!" he said. "He has the hardest job in the world. Won't I cheer him when I next see him! But I wouldn't be in *his* shoes for anything!"

The goblin and the dragon

Once upon a time there was a green goblin called Crooky. He was just like his name, as crooked a goblin as ever lived in Little Town. He didn't tell the truth, he took things belonging to other people, and he was the worst tale-teller anyone could imagine.

No one liked him, no one smiled at him and no one asked him out to tea. Crooky hadn't a single friend, and didn't want one. He was only welcomed by witches, because he sometimes captured prisoners for them to make into servants. He was paid well for that, and was very rich.

Up on the hill behind Little Town was a deep cave. In this cave lived Goofle

the dragon. He was quite harmless, but once in a while he would get terribly hungry; then all the pixies and brownies and goblins kept out of his way till he had fed on the cartful of bananas that the Lord High Chamberlain sent him as soon as he knew the dragon was hungry again. It was said that Goofle might forget his liking for bananas and eat a pixie, if one was near at that time.

Crooky often saw the dragon, because the goblin's house was near the cave. But Goofle didn't like Crooky at all, and wouldn't speak to him. He knew that he was a bad goblin and even dragons like to choose their friends.

This made Crooky very cross, and he was always trying to get Goofle to be friendly with him, so that he might be able to say, "The dragon asked me to tea in his cave," or "The dragon had a picnic with me yesterday," as the other little folk did. But Goofle turned his head away and sniffed loudly whenever Crooky came near, and wouldn't have anything to do with him at all.

Now one day Crooky went to a meeting to hear what arrangements were to be made to greet the King when he came on his yearly visit to Little Town. A pixie and an elf began to quarrel, and all the others tried to stop them.

"Be quiet, Flip!" cried the brownies near by. "You look as ugly as the old dragon when you frown like that!"

"Don't lose your temper, Gobo!" cried the pixies to the elf. "You will grow as ugly as the dragon if you do!"

Now as soon as Crooky heard them calling out these things, a plan came into his mind. Suppose he went to tell the dragon that the little folk called him ugly, surely Goofle would be pleased with him, and would be so angry with the other folk that he would go into the town and eat them all up. Then he and Goofle would be friends, and perhaps the dragon would make Crooky King of Little Town.

"Now, that's a good idea of mine," said Crooky to himself, and he slipped out of the meeting-hall to think about it. "I will pretend to be very much grieved to think that anyone should call Goofle ugly, and I will tell him he is beautiful, and that he should punish those who think he is not. He will be my friend after that, and everything will be lovely."

So the very next day Crooky started out to the dragon's cave. Goofle was lying out in the sun, having a sun-bathe. He was not beautiful – indeed he really was very ugly, for he had scales all over his body, a long spiky tail, and when he breathed, smoke came out of his nose.

"Hello, Goofle," said Crooky, in a very cheerful friendly voice. The dragon took no notice of him, and pretended not to see or hear him.

"*Hello, Goofle!*" shouted Crooky. "I say, I've got something to tell you. You *will* be surprised to hear it. It's something I've heard about you, and you won't be a bit pleased to hear what people say about you. As I feel very friendly towards you, I thought it was my duty to tell you."

Goofle said nothing. He yawned very widely, and shut his eyes. Then, quite suddenly he felt terribly hungry. Once every fifty days he felt like that, and it just happened to be the fiftieth day that morning. He wondered whether the Lord High Chamberlain was sending his cartful of bananas, and he opened his eyes to look down the hill to see if it was coming.

But it wasn't. The Lord High Chamberlain had made a mistake for once, and thought that it was only the forty-ninth day. The bananas were ordered for the next day instead.

Crooky the goblin didn't know that it was the fiftieth day. He went quite near to the dragon and spoke to him once more.

"Do listen, Goofle," he said. "I have something surprising to tell you. Do you know that everyone calls you ugly? What do you think of that?"

Goofle put his paw behind his ear, and pretended that he was hard of hearing, though he could quite well hear every word that the horrid little goblin was saying.

"Come nearer," he said. "I'm deaf in one ear and can't hear out of the other. Come nearer, Crooky!"

So Crooky came nearer.

"Sit on the end of my tail, Crooky," said the dragon. "I'm terribly deaf this morning. Sit on my tail."

So the little tell-tale sat on the end of the dragon's spiky tail, and began to speak again.

"People down in Little Town say that you are very ugly," he said. "I think you ought to eat people that say unkind things about you. I think you are very beautiful."

Goofle pretended he still couldn't hear.

"Sit on my back," he said. "There's a buzzing in one of my ears and a singing noise in the other. I can't hear what you say. Sit on my back, Crooky."

So Crooky sat on the dragon's back, and began to shout. But Goofle only shook his head.

"One ear's deaf and the other's no good," he said. "Sit on my head, Crooky, sit on my head."

So Crooky sat on the dragon's head, and began to shout again. But still it didn't seem to make the dragon hear.

"Sit on my big front tooth, Crooky," he said. "Sit on my big front tooth."

So Crooky sat on the dragon's big front tooth – and then Goofle opened his mouth very wide indeed, jerked back his head, and shut his teeth with a snap.

Where was Crooky? He was gone! The dragon smiled a wide smile, and felt that he could wait for his bananas now. In the distance he saw two or three brownies and he called to them.

"Ho there, brownies!" he cried. "Come here a moment. Crooky said you call me ugly. I hope that that is true. You *do* think I'm ugly, don't you?"

"Of course we do," said the brownies, in surprise. "We have always told you so, Goofle. There isn't such a thing as a beautiful dragon, as you very well know. It is right for you to be ugly."

"I thought so," said Goofle with a pleased sigh. "That stupid Crooky called me beautiful, and it made me feel so angry. I couldn't *bear* to be a beautiful dragon! Why, everyone would laugh at me!"

"Where is Crooky now?" asked the

brownies, looking round. "We will scold him for trying to tell tales. He is the horridest goblin that ever lived!"

The dragon went red, and hung his head.

"Well, you see," he said. "Crooky sat on my big front tooth – and when I opened my mouth, he fell down my throat. I'm afraid you won't see him any more."

"Good gracious!" cried the brownies in a fright. "Why, it must be the fiftieth day! We must go and see about your bananas!"

Off they scurried and sent a message to the Lord High Chamberlain begging him to send the bananas at once. Then they went to tell the news about Crooky to everyone in Little Town.

Nobody said they were sorry, and nobody said they were glad – but Little Town was *ever* so much nicer without Crooky! As for Goofle the dragon, he ate up every one of his bananas, and then went to sleep very happy.

Funny little Shorty

B obby brought a new toy home with him one night. He put it in the toy cupboard.

"There you are, little cat," he said. "Make friends with all my other toys!"

He shut the cupboard door and went off to bed. The toys stared at the new toy in silence. What would he be like?

"Hallo!" said the new toy. "Let's go out and have a run round the playroom, shall we? I'd like to see my new home."

They all went out into the big playroom. It was a nice place, with rugs over the linoleum. "Ha, good!" said the new toy, and he gave a little run and then slid all the way along the slippery linoleum on his four black legs.

"You don't do things like that until we know you better," said Rosebud, the big doll.

"Oh dear – sorry!" said the new toy, and he sat down on the nearby rug. "How long will it take for you to know me better? There's not much to know about me, really."

"What are you?" asked the pink rabbit.

"Well – can't you see! I'm a cat, of course," said the new toy.

"You're not," said the toy dog at once. "You haven't got a tail. All cats have tails."

"Not the kind of cat I am," said the cat. "I'm a Manx toy cat – and Manx cats don't have long tails."

"I don't believe you," said the toy monkey, swinging his lovely, long tail. "You're just saying that to make us think it's all right for you not to have a tail. You must have lost your tail somewhere. Don't tell stories!"

"I am *not*," said the little Manx cat,

crossly. "I never tell stories. I'm telling you the truth. I'm a little Manx cat, and Manx cats don't have tails – or only just a stump, like mine. Do believe me."

But they didn't. They only laughed at the little toy cat. "We shall call you Shorty, because your tail is so very, very short that you almost haven't got one," said the monkey. "You look silly, Shorty. You ought to try and get a tail somewhere. One like mine!"

"I don't want a tail," said Shorty. "I should feel strange with one. I tell you I'm the kind of cat that doesn't have one. So, I don't want one. Is there a teddy bear here? Yes, I can see him. Well, he hasn't got a tail either – but you don't laugh at *him*."

"No, because he's not *supposed* to have one, so he looks all right without one," said the toy dog, wagging his tail to show how strong it was. "You just look silly without one. All cats have tails."

Shorty gave up. "All right," he said.

"Have it your own way. But let me tell you this – I think you're all rather silly and very unkind. I do think you might be more friendly to a new toy."

But the toys weren't nice to Shorty. They turned away from him and wouldn't show him round the playroom. They didn't talk to him much either, and they never asked him to join in their games. He was very sad about it.

"I can't help not having a tail," he thought. "What difference does a tail make? I wish I lived in the Isle of Man where it's strange for a cat to *have* a tail. Oh well – I must just make the best of things."

So Shorty didn't quarrel or grumble. He was always cheerful and smiling and willing to do anything for anyone. He was even glad to wind up the clockwork mouse when the others got tired of it.

"It's a pity you haven't a long, long tail like mine, Shorty," the mouse said each time the toy cat wound him up. "You do look odd, you know."

"Rubbish!" said Shorty, cheerfully. "There you are – your key won't turn any more, so you are fully wound up. Run along."

Now one day a really dreadful thing happened. A little girl came to tea with Bobby, and they quarrelled. Bobby wouldn't let her take his mother's scissors from her work-basket and use them to cut pictures out of his books.

"No, Jennifer," he said. "For one thing I'm not allowed to have those scissors, and nor are you. And for another thing I won't let you spoil my books. You spoil your own, I know – but I *like* my books."

Jennifer was angry. She was a spoilt, loud-voiced little girl, and she shouted at Bobby.

"You're a meanie, that's what you are! A MEANIE! I don't like you. I'll break your train!"

"No, you won't," said Bobby, and he took his train and went into the bedroom. He locked it up in a drawer and came back. While he had gone Jennifer had run to the work-basket and taken the scissors. Her mean little eyes gleamed. She would pay Bobby back for doing that!

"Go and see what the time is," she said to Bobby. "I think it must be getting late."

Bobby went down to the hall to look at the big grandfather clock there. He hoped it *was* getting late, then this horrid girl would go.

Jennifer waited until he was out of the room, then she ran to the toy cupboard and opened it. She pulled out the monkey, the toy dog, the clockwork mouse, the little kangaroo that could jump, and the lovely little horse with his long, long tail.

And what do you think she did? She cut off all their tails! Then she stuffed the toys back into the cupboard, and put the tails in her pocket. She heard Bobby coming back and hurriedly put the scissors into her pocket too. The sharp end stuck into her and hurt her. She began to cry.

"What's the matter?" said Bobby. But Jennifer couldn't tell him, of course. She just said she wanted to go home, and off she went, wondering what Bobby would say when he saw his spoilt toys.

Bobby didn't see them that evening – but, oh dear, what an upset there was when the toys streamed out of the cupboard that night! How they cried.

Shorty was very sorry for them all, because he knew how much they thought of their tails. He tried to comfort them.

"Cheer up. Perhaps we can make other tails, just as nice as yours. Don't cry."

"Don't be silly," said the monkey. "Where can we get new tails!"

"I can find *you* one," said Shorty, and he pointed to where the curtain was looped back with a long silk plait. "A bit of that would look fine on you!"

"So it would," said Monkey, wiping his

eyes. In a trice Shorty had snipped a piece off the curtain loop, and had given it to Rosebud to sew on to Monkey.

"Find me a tail, find *me* a tail!" begged the little clockwork mouse, running up to him.

"There's a very nice piece of black string in the string-box," said Shorty. "It would make you a wonderful tail!"

And it did. You should have seen the clockwork mouse with his new black tail. It was even longer than his old one.

Shorty was very clever. He found an old furry collar belonging to Rosebud the doll. She said she didn't want it, so he carefully cut it up into two pieces, and made tails for the toy dog and the kangaroo. They were simply delighted.

"My new tail wags better than the old one," said the toy dog and he wagged it.

"What about me, please, Shorty?" neighed the little horse. "My tail was so beautiful – it was made of hairs, you know."

"Yes, I know," said Shorty, thoughtfully. "Now, let me see – what would be best for *your* tail? Oh, I know! What about taking some hairs from the old rug by the fireplace?"

So he pulled twenty hairs from the rug and neatly tied them together. Then Rosebud sewed on the new tail and the little horse swished it about in delight.

"You're very, very kind," said the monkey, in rather a small voice.

"Yes, you are," said all the toys.

"You've bothered about new tails for us," said the toy dog, "but you haven't even *thought* of one for yourself. We've teased you and teased you – and instead of being glad when we had no tails, like you, you were sorry and made some for us. Do, do make yourself a tail, too."

"No, don't," said Rosebud, suddenly. "I like you without a tail, Shorty. I do really. You wouldn't be Shorty if you had a tail!"

"But wouldn't you all like me better

with one?" said Shorty, surprised. "I *could* make one, of course. I just didn't think of it for myself."

"No, Shorty, no!" cried all the toys, and the little kangaroo came and hugged him. "We like you as you are. It's funny – but you look *nice* without a tail. Don't have one! You wouldn't be our nice old Shorty!"

Shorty beamed all over his whiskery face. "All right," he said. "I won't have one. I don't want one, because I'm not supposed to wear a tail, anyway! Well – are we all going to be good friends now?"

"Yes – if you'll have us," said the pink rabbit, looking rather ashamed of himself. "And listen, Shorty, if anyone is ever unkind to you again, just go and pull his tail!"

"All right," said Shorty, with a grin. "But I shan't need to!"

And he didn't, of course. They were all good friends after that – but Bobby *is* puzzled about all the new tails!

The very strange pool

Now once upon a time Shiny-One the gnome had to take a heavy mirror to Dame Pretty. It was a very large looking-glass indeed, bigger than Shiny-One himself, so it made him puff and pant, as you can imagine.

When he got to the middle of Cuckoo Wood he felt that he really *must* have a rest. So he laid the mirror flat on the ground, with the bracken and grass peeping into it, and went to lean against a tree a little way off. And he fell fast asleep.

Now along that way came little Peep and Pry, the two naughty little boy pixies who lived at the edge of the wood. They were always peeping and prying into things that were no business of theirs – so you can guess they were most astonished to see a big flat shining thing in the middle of the wood!

"Look at that!" said Peep. "A pool!"

"A lovely, shiny pool!" said Pry. They both ran to it – and indeed, the mirror did look exactly like a shining pool of clear water, for it reflected the grass, the bracken, the trees and the sky, exactly as a sheet of water does.

"I wonder how a pool suddenly came here," said Peep. "It's really rather extraordinary. There was never one here before."

"It hasn't been raining," said Pry. "I just can't understand it. Do you suppose it is a magic pool, Peep?"

"Yes – perhaps it is," said Peep.

"Peep – shall we take a little drink from it, in case it's a wishing-pool?" whispered Pry.

"Well – do you think we'd better?" said Peep. "Suppose it belongs to somebody?"

"They'll never know," said naughty Pry. "Come on – let's scoop a little water up in our hands and drink it. We'll wish at the same time."

Peep put his hand down to the mirror – but, of course, all he felt was something hard, and not soft water!

"The pool's frozen!" he said. "Look — there's no water — only ice."

"Well, that *shows* it's magic!" said Pry at once. "That just shows it is! How could water freeze on a warm autumn day like this? It's impossible."

"I think you're right," said Peep in excitement. "Yes, I really think you are. A pool that is frozen hard on a warm day *must* be magic! Whoever it belongs to must have frozen it so that nobody could take a drink and wish."

"Ah — but we can manage to trick the owner!" said Pry in a whisper. "We can break the ice, Peep — and drink the water below! Can't we?"

"Of course!" said Peep. "Come on — let's break it and drink quickly, before anyone comes."

So they took stones and banged the pool hard — crack! The mirror broke into little pieces — and to the pixies' great astonishment there was no water underneath!

"Stranger and stranger!" said Peep. "I wish there was somebody we could tell this to."

Then they saw Shiny-One, the gnome, not very far off. He was just waking up. They ran to him.

"I say, there's a magic pool over there!" said Peep.

"We knew it was magic, because it was frozen hard," added Pry. "So we cracked the ice to get a drink of the water underneath – but there wasn't any! Did you ever know such magic?"

"What nonsense are you talking?" said Shiny-One crossly. He knew Peep and Pry well and didn't like the way they poked their noses into things that had nothing to do with them. "A magic pool – frozen on a day like this! Rubbish!"

Peep and Pry took him to the pool – and Shiny-One stared down in horror at his poor broken mirror.

"My mirror!" he said. "The one I was selling to Dame Pretty. Look what you've done, with your silly interfering ways – smashed that beautiful big mirror! You bad pixies! How much money have you got in your pockets? You'll have to pay for that mirror!"

Peep and Pry tried to run away – but Shiny-One caught hold of them both. He turned them upside down and shook them well. All their money rolled out of their pockets.

"Thank you," said Shiny-One, and he turned the pixies the right way up. "Thank you! Just enough to pay for a new mirror, I think. Now run off before I think of smacking you both."

Peep and Pry ran off, crying. Shiny-One dug a hole with a stick and buried all the bits of broken mirror, so that nobody's feet would get cut.

As for poor Peep and Pry, they had to go without buying sweets for four weeks, because all their money had gone – so maybe they won't go poking their noses about quite so much another time!

Mr Stamp-About again

Mr Stamp-About went to stay with his aunt, Miss Prim, and his uncle, Mr Hearty. They asked him for Christmas, and said he could stay until the New Year was in.

"Thanks very much," said Mr Stamp-About, pleased. "I should have been all alone if you hadn't asked me. I'll come with pleasure."

He packed up his things. Mr Cheery from next door helped him to carry them to the station.

"Now you have a good time, Stamp-About," he said, "and just remember that when you stay with people you have to put on your best behaviour — so no stamping about and shouting!"

"Don't you talk to me like that!" said Stamp-About, glaring. "Do you suppose I don't know how to behave?"

"Well, that's just what I do suppose," said Cheery. "*I* heard you stamping round the kitchen roaring at your cat this morning. She came flying out of the window like a streak of lightning!"

Stamp-About opened his mouth to roar at Cheery, but the train came in and roared even louder. He got in and Cheery banged the door. "Happy Christmas!" he said, "and don't forget to make some good resolutions for the New Year!"

Well, Stamp-About really did have a lovely Christmas and enjoyed himself very much. He stayed till the New Year, and on New Year's Eve, when he was in bed, he made all kinds of very good resolutions, just as you do. You know what good resolutions are, of course — you make up your mind to do this and do that all through the New Year, and not to do the things you know you shouldn't.

"I shall keep my temper," thought Stamp-About. "I shall not shout or yell. I shall not stamp my feet. I shall not be rude. I shall, in fact, be quite a different person. Dear me, how interesting it will be."

He fell asleep feeling pleased and happy. How easy it was to make good resolutions – and what a fine lot he had made.

Now, the next day Mr Cheery came along to help him back home with his luggage, and he brought his cheeky little nephew, Smarty, with him. Mr Stamp-About looked at Smarty, and he didn't like him.

"Well, Smarty," said Miss Prim, "this is New Year's Day. I am sure you have made all kinds of good resolutions."

"Yes, Miss Prim," said Smarty. "But I bet Mr Stamp-About hasn't."

"No, I don't suppose he has," said Mr Hearty. "Stamp-About, I've never known you make a good New Year's resolution yet! You'd have got rid of that bad temper of yours if you had!"

"*Ha ha!*" said Mr Cheery, "why, I wouldn't know old Stamp-About without his temper! He loses it so often that I really think he must spend his days finding it again! *Ha ha!*"

"That's not funny," said Mr Stamp-About, glaring at him.

"*I* think it's funny," said Smarty, and laughed so much that he fell over. "You want to keep your temper tied up like a dog, Mr Stamp-About. Then you wouldn't lose it. That could be one of your good resolutions – buy lead and collar for temper, and tie it up. *Ha ha ha!*"

"If Stamp-About wanted to make any good resolutions I could tell him plenty," said Uncle Hearty. "Now, now – don't look so upset, Stamp-About. We're only teasing you."

"Then don't," said Stamp-About, going very red in the face. "I don't mind telling you that I've made more good resolutions this New Year than all of you people put together. So there!"

Everyone laughed. Cheery poked him in the ribs. "Don't boast, old fellow — and, anyway, I can guess what your resolutions are — shout at the cat, yell at the dog, moan at everybody, and. . . ."

"How *dare* you say that!" yelled Mr Stamp-About, losing his temper very suddenly indeed. "Poking your great silly nose into my affairs! Telling me not to boast! *I* don't boast. You're the one who boasts. And as for that silly nephew of yours, if he doesn't take that stupid grin off his face, I'll make him stand outside in the cold!"

"What behaviour!" said Miss Prim, shocked. "Apologise to Smarty, Stamp-About."

"Certainly not!" roared Stamp-About, and he stamped his foot so hard that all the ornaments on the mantelpiece jumped. "Getting at me like this! I won't have it. No, I won't."

He stamped round the room, fuming, and shook his big fist right under

Smarty's nose. "*Grrrrrrr*!" he roared.

"Now, now," said Miss Prim, shocked, "aren't you forgetting this is New Year? What a pity you didn't make a few really good resolutions, Stamp-About!"

Stamp-About went purple. He roared at his aunt. "I tell you I *did* make some good resolutions. Plenty. More than anybody. *Ha*! You don't believe me, do you?"

"Well, tell us them, then maybe we *will* believe you," said Cheery.

"Right!" shouted Stamp-About, with an enormous frown. "Well, here they are – and jolly good ones, too. I made up my mind to keep my temper. And not to shout or yell. Not to stamp my feet. And not to be rude. So there! *Now* do you believe me?"

And he stamped his foot again, and made the clock suddenly strike twelve before it ought to.

Everyone began to laugh. Cheery pointed his finger at the angry Stamp-About. "I'll die of laughing, Stamp-

About, I really will! Did you forget that good resolutions have to be *kept*? Don't you know that. . . ."

But Stamp-About was gone, and they heard him stamping down the garden path without his stick or his paper or his luggage. "*Pah*!" they heard him say. "*Pah*! That's the last time *I* ever make New Year resolutions!"

Poor old Stamp-About! He didn't know that although they were so very easy to make they're always hard to keep. *I've* found that out already, haven't you?

The rough little boy

Anna was to go to tea with her Auntie Susan. She loved her aunt, and was very pleased to be going all alone down the street to see her.

"I shall take her the beautiful bead necklace I was making for her yesterday," said Anna happily. "She will like that. And, Mummy, can I wear my lovely new red hair-ribbon?"

"Yes, you can," said Mummy, and she got the ribbon out of the box. She brushed Anna's hair, and tied the new red ribbon on one side. It did look nice. "I shall carry the bead necklace in my hand," said Anna. "Then I can look at it. It is so pretty. There are beads of all colours, Mummy – red, blue, green, yellow, brown and white. Do you think Auntie Susan will like it?"

"She will love it," said Mummy. "Now be careful to keep on the path, Anna, and don't go into the road at all. You don't need a hat. Run along now and come home again at six o'clock."

So off Anna went. She felt very proud of the red ribbon in her hair and very proud of the bead necklace in her hand. It had taken her a long time to thread. The beads were nice and big, made of coloured glass, and they shone brightly in the sun.

Just round the corner Anna saw a boy she didn't like a bit! It was Thomas, and he was rough. He was the kind of boy who loved to pull little girls' hair, and to snatch off little boys' caps. I expect you know the kind of boy. Nobody likes them much.

Well, there came Thomas, whistling loudly and looking for mischief. And as soon as he saw Anna he grinned. Ah, here was a little girl to tease!

He ran up to her. "What have you got in your hand?" he asked.

"Never mind," said Anna, and she put her hand behind her.

"Let me see," said Thomas, and he tried to open her hand. He hurt Anna, and the little girl had to open her fingers. The necklace fell to the pavement, the string broke, and the lovely beads rolled all over the place!

"You horrid, horrid boy!" cried Anna, with tears in her eyes. "I made that for my Auntie Susan. Help me to pick up the beads."

She bent down to pick them up – and Thomas caught sight of the new red ribbon. He snatched at it – and it came off. Then away went Thomas with the ribbon flying in his fingers, calling, "Here goes your red ribbon! Here goes your red ribbon!"

Anna didn't know whether to run after her ribbon or pick up her beads. She stood there with tears rolling down her cheeks. The horrid rude boy! He had

got her ribbon and broken her necklace.

"Here goes your red ribbon!" cried Thomas, and he flapped it at Anna down the road as he ran. He didn't look where he was going and he ran straight into a lamp-post. Down he went and banged his head hard against the post. How he yelled and cried!

Anna ran to help him. She pulled Thomas to his feet and wiped his hands clean. She looked at his hurt knee and tied it up with her handkerchief. He looked very red and ashamed when she had finished.

"Thank you," he said. "How funny of you to help somebody who teased you!"

"I still think you are a horrid little boy," said Anna, "but we have to help even horrid people if they are in trouble. You'd better go home to your mother. But give me back my red ribbon first."

"It's gone," said Thomas, looking all round for it. "Quite gone. The wind must have blown it away. I say – I'm really sorry."

"Well, you might help me to pick up my beads," said Anna, who meant to make Thomas do something. "I am very, very sad about my new ribbon. I'm going to tea with my Auntie, and she will think I'm most untidy without a ribbon in my hair."

Thomas went back down the street to

pick up the beads. He got a handful of them and then looked at Anna.

"Have you got a pocket to put them in?" he asked.

"No," said Anna. "I even have to keep my hanky up my sleeve. Oh dear! How shall I carry the beads?"

"I live just here," said Thomas, going into a nearby gate. "Come in and I'll see if I've got a box to put the beads in for you."

Anna went inside the gate and waited for Thomas. Presently he came out carrying an old chocolate box. It was very pretty indeed, and had a picture of a kitten on the front and a big piece of blue ribbon round the lid.

"Here you are," said Thomas, opening the box. "You can have this box. It's my best chocolate box, and I kept my marbles in it. But you can have it for helping me. Truly I am sorry I broke your necklace."

"Oh, thank you," said Anna, and she put all her beads into the chocolate box.

They made a nice rattly sound. "Well, I really don't mind about the necklace now, because I have this lovely box — and I can easily thread all the beads again. But it's a shame about my ribbon. I do hate going out to tea without a ribbon in my hair."

"I say! What about taking the ribbon off the chocolate box lid!" cried Thomas, pointing to the broad blue ribbon that went round the lid. He pulled it off and held it up. It was a fine piece, wide and silky and blue. "It's just right for you," said Thomas. "Your eyes are blue and the ribbon is blue! Can you tie it on?"

"I think so," said Anna. She put down her chocolate box and took the ribbon. She tied it neatly on her hair in a big bow. It did look nice.

"Anna, it's *much* prettier than the red ribbon!" said Thomas. And so it was. Anna looked lovely with it on her hair. She felt very pleased.

"Well, goodbye, Thomas," she said. "You may be a horrid, rough little boy, but you're quite nice and kind, too. I like that part of you."

"Will you come and play with me tomorrow?" asked Thomas. "I promise I won't be rough. You can keep my chocolate box for your very own."

"I'll ask my mother if I can come and play," said Anna. "Goodbye! What a lot I shall have to tell my Auntie Susan!"

And off she went with the blue ribbon in her hair and the chocolate box under her arm, the beads rattling gaily.

"Well, what a good thing I was kind to Thomas when he fell down," thought Anna. "I would never, never have known that he was anything but a very horrid, rough little boy. I think I *will* go and play with him tomorrow if Mummy says yes. And I might even give him my tiny blue car – if he isn't rough again!"

Well, Thomas has got the blue car – so he couldn't have been rough. It was a good thing for him that he met a kind child like Anna, wasn't it?

Bottom of the class!

Somebody always has to be at the bottom of every class. "But," said Miss Brown, "it needn't always be the *same* person, Bobby!"

You see, Bobby was *always* at the bottom. He was very sorry about it, but he couldn't help it. He had been ill for two years of his school life, and that meant that he was far behind everyone else.

He wasn't very good at handiwork, either, because he was left-handed, and that seemed to make him awkward with the raffia or the cane that the class used to make baskets.

He was bad at games because he wasn't strong and couldn't run fast.

His mother was often very sorry for the little boy, because he never once grumbled or complained, and yet she knew he must be unhappy about it.

There was one thing that Bobby was very, very fond of, and that was gardening. He might not be able to run fast, but you should see him weeding! And the flowers didn't mind whether he was left-handed or right-handed, because he always knew when to water them, when to weed, and when to tie them up so that the wind couldn't blow them down.

"You know, Daddy," his mother said to his father, "Bobby isn't much good at anything except gardening. So we must help him all we can with that. When people aren't much good at anything, and can't help it, it's very important to find *something* they like and can do really well. And gardening is what Bobby likes best of all."

So his parents gave Bobby a very big piece of the garden. They bought him a spade and fork, watering-can, trowels, dibbers, raffia for tying, and a fine wheelbarrow. He was delighted.

"Oh, *thank* you!" he said. "Now I'll really be able to grow marvellous flowers. And, Mummy, do you know what I shall do? I shall grow enough flowers for you to have them all over the house, and enough to take to Miss Brown twice a week to keep our classroom beautiful. Then she'll know that even if I'm at the bottom of the class and stay there, I can at least *do something!*"

He kept his word. He worked hard in his garden each day. He dug, he weeded, he sowed, he watered. He thinned out his seedlings, he put soot down to keep away slugs, he tied up his tall plants so that the wind should not break them.

And all the term his mother had her house full of flowers from Bobby's garden, and, really, you should have seen Bobby's classroom! There were roses on the mantelpiece, lupins on the window-sill, pinks on the bookcase smelling as sweet as sugar. Miss Brown said they never had so many lovely flowers, and all the children were grateful to Bobby and his gardening.

The summer term went on. There was to be a concert and a handiwork show at the end. Bobby wasn't in anything at the concert, except in the opening song, because he simply couldn't remember the words in any play or recitation for more than a day. He couldn't even sing in tune, so Miss Brown told him not to sing too loudly in the opening song, in case he put the others off.

Bobby was the only child who had nothing on show in the handiwork display. He had been trying to make a basket, like the others, but it was so bad that Miss Brown said she was sorry, but she couldn't possibly show it.

The lady at the big house was to come to hear the concert and open the show.

But on the day before the concert she fell ill and couldn't come. The children were sorry, because they liked her. But she sent rather an exciting message. "I have asked a friend of mine to come instead," she said. "She is a duchess, so I hope you will welcome her nicely and thank her properly for coming."

"A duchess!" said the children. "Goodness, Miss Brown – we'll all have to be extra smart, and won't we have to present her with a bouquet – a really beautiful bunch of flowers?"

"Yes, we shall," said Miss Brown. "I must order some at once. Now – who shall give the flowers to her?"

The top girl of the class felt certain *she* would be chosen. The boy who happened to be games captain just then hoped *he* would be. Suzette, the smartest girl in the class, remembered her beautiful new silk frock, and thought *she* ought to be the one to curtsey and present the flowers.

But suddenly little Mary spoke up. "Miss Brown, *I* think Bobby ought to present the bouquet! Look at all the lovely flowers he's grown for us this term. He ought to have some reward – and he's not doing anything special in the concert, and he's got nothing in the handiwork show. I do think he ought to present the flowers."

There was a moment's silence and then all the children – yes, even the top girl, the games captain and Suzette – shouted out loudly: "Yes! *yes*! That's fair. Let Bobby do it! Let Bobby give the flowers!"

What an honour for Bobby. He sat blushing in his seat, his eyes shining. What would his mother say when she saw him going up to the Duchess and bowing and presenting the bouquet? Bobby was as glad for his mother as he was for himself.

It was all settled – except that Bobby insisted that he should bring the bouquet from his own garden. "I've got the loveliest carnations and roses this week you ever saw," he said. "Better than in any of the shops. Real beauties – and I'd love to give them to the Duchess."

So Bobby picked his carnations and roses, made them into a magnificent bouquet, and took them to school the next afternoon. All the mothers were there, and some of the fathers. It was a great day for the school and the parents.

The pretty Duchess drove up in a lovely black car. The children cheered. She smiled and went up on to the little platform to speak to the children.

And then, very proudly, Bobby went up on to the platform, too, carrying the flowers he had grown himself. He looked neat and tidy, his hair was well brushed, his shoes shone, and his nails were clean. Miss Brown was proud of him.

Bobby bowed and presented the bouquet to the Duchess. His mother almost cried for joy. The Duchess took the flowers and exclaimed over them: "How beautiful! I have never, never had such a wonderful bouquet before!

Oh, thank you. What *glorious* roses and carnations!"

Little Mary couldn't stop herself from calling out: "Bobby grew them himself! He picked them out of his own garden for you!"

"Good gracious! What a clever boy you must be!" said the Duchess. "How proud your school must be of you!"

Bobby was as red as a beetroot. He almost burst for joy. He was at the bottom of the form and always had been – and here he was being told he was clever by the Duchess herself – and he *knew* the school was proud of him!

So they were. They were proud of him and they liked him. As for his mother, how she beamed when all the other mothers crowded round her afterwards, and praised her Bobby!

Bobby's grown up now. He is the head of a very fine flower-growing firm. He takes all the prizes there are. It's surprising what you can do, even if you *are* at the bottom of the class!

The dirty old teddy

Once there was an old, old teddy bear in the toy cupboard. He was so old and dirty that nobody knew what colour he had once been, and he didn't even remember himself.

He only had one arm, and one of his legs was loose. His eyes were odd, because one was a black button and the other was brown. He had a hole in his back and sawdust sometimes came out of it. So you can guess he was rather a poor old thing.

But he was wise and kind and loved to make a joke, so the other toys loved him and didn't mind him being so dirty and old.

"All the same, I'm afraid he'll be

thrown away into the dustbin one day," said the blue rabbit, shaking his head. "I'm afraid he will. He really is *so* old and dirty."

The little girl in whose playroom the bear lived never played with the old teddy. She had a fine new one, coloured blue, with a pink ribbon round his neck, two beautiful eyes, and a growl in his middle. She loved him very much. She always pushed the old teddy away if he was near her.

One day her mother picked up the old teddy and looked at him. A little

sawdust dribbled out of the hole in his back.

"Good gracious!" said Joan's mother. "This old teddy really must be thrown away. He isn't even nice enough to be given to the jumble sale."

"Well, throw him away, then," said Joan. "I don't want him. He looks horrid with only one arm and a leg that wobbles, Mummy. I never play with him now."

All the toys listened in horror. What! Throw away the poor old teddy! Oh, dear, what a terrible pity!

"Well, I'll put him in the waste-paper basket in a minute," said her mother. She put the teddy on the table beside her and went on with her knitting. Soon the bell rang for dinner, and Joan's mother forgot about the teddy.

As soon as she had gone out of the room the toys called to the bear, "Hurry, Teddy! Get down from the table and hide at the back of the toy cupboard!"

The bear fell off the table and limped

over to the toy cupboard. He really was very frightened. He hoped that Joan's mother wouldn't remember she had left him on the table.

She didn't remember – because when she came back she had another child with her, besides Joan. A little boy clung to her hand, and she was talking to him.

"You will love staying with us, Peter dear. You shall play with Joan's toys, and have a ride on the rocking-horse."

Peter was Joan's cousin and he had come to stay with Joan for three weeks. He was a dear little boy, but very shy. The toys watched him all the afternoon. He was frightened of the rocking-horse because it was so big. He liked the dolls' house because everything in it was little. He loved the top that spun round and played a tune, and he liked the train that ran on its lines.

When bedtime came, and he sat eating bread-and-milk in the playroom, he began to cry.

"I've left my old monkey behind," he wept. "I always go to bed with him. I shall be lonely without him."

"Well, you shall have one of Joan's toys to take to bed with you," said her mother, and she took him to the toy cupboard. "Choose which you would like, Peter."

Peter picked up the brown dog – and then the rabbit – and then the sailor doll – and then the blue cat. And then, quite suddenly, he saw the dirty old teddy bear looking up at him out of his odd brown and black eyes. He gave a squeal and picked him up.

"Oh, can I have this darling soft teddy? He looks at me so kindly – and I do like his funny eyes. Oh, please, please, may I take *him* to bed with me?"

"Good gracious! It's the bear I meant to throw away in the dustbin!" said Joan's mother. "You don't want a dirty old toy like that, surely!"

"Yes I do – yes I do!" cried Peter, and he hugged the bear hard. "I shall cry if you don't let me have him."

"Of course you shall have him, but if you love him so much I shall have to mend him up a bit tomorrow," said Joan's mother. So Peter took the old teddy to bed with him – and you simply can't imagine how happy the bear was! He cuddled up to Peter and loved him. It was such a long, long time since he had been taken to bed by anyone. He was so happy that even his little growl came back when Peter pressed his tummy.

And next day – good gracious! Joan's mother took him and made him a new arm. She sewed on his wobbly leg. She mended the hole in his back – and she made him a beautiful blue shirt with little sleeves!

You can't think how different he looked! The other toys looked at him in amazement and joy.

"You won't go into the dustbin now, Teddy," they said. "You look simply lovely!"

The day the Princess came

"The Princess is coming to visit our village!" shouted Bron the brownie, racing through the streets, waving a letter. "Next week! Hurray! She wants to have tea in one of our cottages! Hurray!"

Well, what an excitement! A meeting was held at once, and all the villagers went to it, of course.

"Now, we must vote for the prettiest, best-kept cottage in our village," said Bron, importantly. "All our cottages are pretty, but not all of them are tidy and clean and well-kept inside. The Princess must have tea in the one that is best inside as well as outside."

So all the villagers voted on bits

of paper and put down the name of the cottage they thought to be the best for the Princess to have tea in.

"I'll count the votes," said Bron, and he did. He looked up, puzzled. "*Two* cottages have exactly the same number of votes!" he said. "Cherry Cottage, where Dame Twinkle lives – and Apple Cottage, where old Mother Quickfeet lives. Exactly the same number of votes each!"

"Well – let the Princess choose which cottage she will have tea in when she comes!" called out Pippitty the pixie. "*We* can't choose. Both cottages are beautiful, inside and out."

So it was left like that – and dear me, how Mother Quickfeet and Dame Twinkle set to work to make their cottages shine and sparkle!

Their gardens were lovely, full of hollyhocks and cornflowers and marigolds and sweet-peas, and there wasn't a weed to be seen. Dame Twinkle got Bron to whitewash her cottage and Mother Quickfeet got Pippitty to paint her shutters a pretty blue.

And dear me, what a lot of work went on inside! Each cottage had just two rooms, a bedroom and a parlour. Up went new curtains, each carpet was beaten till it could have cried, and the floors were polished till they were like mirrors. New cushion-covers were made, flowers were set in every corner, the windows were cleaned over and over again, and the smell of freshly baked pies came out of the open doors of the cottages, and made everyone wish they could go and taste them!

That was the day before the Princess was to visit the village. People came and peeped inside the two cottages, wondering which one the Princess would choose.

"I *think* she'll choose Mother Quickfeet's," said Bron. "She has such a pretty wallpaper, so fresh and flowery."

"Ah, but Dame Twinkle has a

rocking-chair," said Pippitty. "I'm sure the Princess would like to sit in that rocking-chair."

Now that night something happened. The cottage next door to Mother Quickfeet's caught fire. It was a little thatched cottage, and soon the straw roof was sending up big flames to the sky. What a to-do!

"Old Man Surly's cottage is burning!" cried Dame Twinkle, when she went out to take in her washing. Just then Mrs Surly rushed into her own garden and called out loudly.

"We can't save the cottage. My children are frightened. So are the cat and the dog. Please, please will you and Mother Quickfeet take us in for the night?"

Then Mother Quickfeet ran out into *her* garden. Dear, dear, what a to-do! Nothing would save that old cottage now. Well, it was tumbling down anyway, and it was all Mr Surly's fault for never doing anything to put it right!

"You can all go to your uncle's," said Mother Quickfeet. "He's got a nice big house, and he'll take you in."

"But it's night-time, and he lives such a long way away," wept Mrs Surly. "And my baby is ill. Oh, please do let us rest in your two cottages tonight, Mother Quickfeet and Dame Twinkle."

Now there were three boys and girls in the Surly family besides the baby – and, alas, they were not very well brought-up children. They were rough and rather rude. As for the dog, he was a dreadful chewer, and everyone shooed him away if they saw him because he would chew up carpets or shoes or books – anything he came across!

"We can't have you," said Mother Quickfeet, firmly. "It's quite impossible. Surely you know that Mother Twinkle and I are hoping to have the Princess to tea tomorrow, and have got our cottages simply beautiful? No – you go to your uncle's. It's your own fault that the cottage has caught fire. You don't sweep the chimney often enough."

Mrs Surly began to cry. The baby howled. The dog barked. Mr Surly growled, and picked up the baby's cradle, which he had managed to save.

"All right," he said. "We'll go. Maybe we can find someone kinder than you, with your talk of beautiful cottages and lovely princesses!"

The little company set off gloomily down the lane. They passed Mother Quickfeet's cottage, and she kept the door shut fast! They passed Dame Twinkle's, too – but before they had gone very far she was out of her door and at the gate calling loudly.

"Mrs Surly! You can come in here. I can't bear to let you walk all that way to your uncle's in the dark of night. Come along in, all of you!"

Mother Quickfeet opened her door. "*Well!*" she said, "fancy having that rough, bad-mannered family to stay with you the night before the Princess arrives! You must be mad!"

"Well – perhaps I am," said Dame Twinkle. "I can't help it. I just feel so sorry for them all. And anyway they'll be gone tomorrow morning and I can easily clear up after them and make things nice again. Are you sure you won't have one or two of the children tonight, Mother Quickfeet? They'll make such a crowd in my cottage."

"Certainly *not*," said Mother Quickfeet and she slammed her door quickly.

Soon all the Surly family was in Cherry Cottage – and dear me, they certainly filled every corner! What with the baby, three other children, Mr and Mrs Surly, *and* the cat and dog, there didn't seem anywhere to sit or even to stand!

Dame Twinkle made them as comfortable as she could. They were all hungry, so she gave them all the pies and cakes and jam sandwiches she had made for the next day.

"I can easily make some more," she thought. "Oh dear – that dog is chewing my new rug. Shoo, dog, shoo!"

The dog shooed away, and began to chew a cushion. The cat leapt up on the mantelpiece and knocked down the clock – smash!

The three children squashed into the lovely rocking-chair and rocked hard. Creak, creak, crash! One of the rockers broke and down went all the children.

"Oh dear – my lovely rocking-chair," said Dame Twinkle, sadly. "Oh, Mrs Surly, *don't* let the baby pull my flowers out of that vase!"

But the baby did, and after that he crawled to the coal-scuttle, and threw bits of coal all over the place! The dog chewed the bits, and then when anyone walked across the room, crunch-crunch went the bits of chewed-up coal under their feet!

Mr Surly lighted his pipe. Goodness gracious, what a smoke he made, and how horrid it smelt! Mother Twinkle almost cried. Would the smell of smoke have gone from the room before the Princess came?

Next morning Mother Quickfeet looked into Dame Twinkle's cottage. My goodness, what a mess! A dirty floor, torn cushions, a chewed-up carpet, a broken rocking-chair, and everything in a mess and a muddle!

Mother Quickfeet didn't say a word. She went back to her own trim and tidy cottage, smiling. Aha! Dame Twinkle wouldn't *dream* of inviting the Princess in now. That was quite certain. She would come to tea with Mother Quickfeet, in Apple Cottage.

After breakfast Mr Surly fetched a big hand barrow from the greengrocer's. He piled on to it the few things saved from the fire. The baby was set on it, too, and the little family set off down the lane to go to their uncle's.

"Goodbye, dear, kind Dame Twinkle," said Mrs Surly, hugging her. "I do wish I could stay and help you to clean up, but if we don't start off now we'll never get there. I shall *never* forget your kindness."

Poor Dame Twinkle. She looked round her little cottage, and almost cried. So dirty. So untidy. So many things broken — even her beloved rocking-chair. Could she ever get things straight in time?

She tried her best. She scrubbed the floor, and when it was dry she polished it. She washed the cushions and mended them. She put the broken clock away. She called in Pippitty to mend the rocking-chair, but he said it would take a whole week.

"What a mess your place is in," he said. "It was very kind of you to take in that poor family — but, oh dear, how sad just before the Princess was arriving! I'm *sure* she would have chosen you to have tea with, Dame Twinkle."

Dame Twinkle looked round the room sadly. "I shan't bother about it any more," she said. "No matter how hard I work I won't have time to get it nice again now. Mother Quickfeet must have the Princess to tea – her cottage really does look lovely."

So Dame Twinkle didn't try to do much more to her cottage. She was tired out with her disturbed night so, after dinner, she changed her dress, and put on her best one, so that she could stand at her front gate and wave to the Princess, when she came.

Cloppetty-cloppetty-clop! That was the sound of horses' hooves. The Princess was coming, hurrah, hurrah, hurrah! All the villagers lined the road and shouted and cheered, for they loved the beautiful, kind-hearted princess.

Along came the carriage, what a beauty! And there was the princess, lovelier than ever, a shining crown on her golden hair. She bowed this way and that, and looked just as pleased as the cheering people.

"Your Royal Highness, Mother

Quickfeet, whose cottage is the prettiest and best of all, begs you to take a cup of tea with her," said Bron the brownie, bowing low. He guided the carriage horses to Apple Cottage. At the gate stood Mother Quickfeet, looking very grand indeed in plum-coloured silk, smiling all over her face.

"Wait," said the Princess. "It is *Cherry* Cottage I want, not Apple Cottage."

"No, no," said Bron, hurriedly. "You're making a mistake, Your Highness. It's *Apple* Cottage!"

"Listen to me," said the Princess, in a little, high voice that everyone could hear. "On my way here I met a little family. The man was pushing a hand barrow, and a baby was crying in the middle of it. I stopped and asked them what they were doing and where they were going. And do you know what they said?"

"What?" asked everyone, crowding close.

"They said they had lost their house in a fire last night and had asked Mother Quickfeet at Apple Cottage to take them in – and she wouldn't. But they said that Dame Twinkle, at Cherry Cottage, called after them and took them all in, every one!"

"Good old Dame Twinkle!" shouted Pippitty.

"Mrs Surly told me they had made a mess of her beautiful cottage, and she said she was very sorry because she knew Dame Twinkle wanted me to go to have tea with her," went on the Princess. "Where *is* this kind Dame Twinkle?"

"Here she is, here she is!" yelled Bron the brownie, in excitement, and showed the Princess where the kind old woman was standing wonderingly at her front gate.

"Oh, please!" Dame Twinkle said, half-scared. "Oh, please, dear Bron, don't ask the Princess in to tea at my house. It's in *such* a mess!"

"Dear Dame Twinkle, I'm not coming to tea with you today!" called the little Princess. "I know how horrid it is to have visitors when your house is untidy. So I'm going to take you home to tea with *me*, back to the palace. Will you come?"

What an honour for Dame Twinkle! No one in the whole village had *ever* gone to tea with a Princess before.

And there was Dame Twinkle stepping into the royal carriage, blushing red, hardly able to speak a word!

"Next week I'll come and have tea with *you*, Dame Twinkle," said the Princess, loud enough for Mother Quickfeet to hear. "Not because you have a pretty cottage, which is a common enough thing – but because you've a warm, kind heart, and that's quite rare! Now – are you quite comfortable? And do you like meringues for tea, because I know we've got some at the palace?"

Nobody heard what Dame Twinkle answered, because the carriage drove off at that moment, clippitty-clop-clop. Everyone cheered again. They didn't mind the Princess paying such a short visit, because she would be back again the next week. Hurrah!

"Good old Dame Twinkle – she deserves a treat," cried Bron. "Three cheers, everyone!"

And every single person joined in – except Mother Quickfeet, who had gone quietly back into her beautiful cottage to cry.

Oh dear – what could she do now? Well – she could go and tidy up Dame Twinkle's cottage, and bake her some pies to welcome her when she came back.

Do you suppose she did? I do hope so.